THE MANUSCRIPTS

THE MANUSCRIPTS

A NOVEL

KEVIN ALLARDICE

LOS ANGELES

Library of Congress Cataloging-in-Publication Data

Names: Allardice, Kevin, author.
Title: The manuscripts : a novel / Kevin Allardice.
Description: Los Angeles : What Books Press, 2024. | Summary: "After
  insinuating himself into the company of a famous philosopher, an art
  student finds himself with an unexpected job. Aided by a driver with
  obscure motives, the student must chaperone the philosopher around the
  countryside to retrieve manuscripts hidden during the recent war. These
  manuscripts, however, reveal more than expected"-- Provided by
  publisher.
Identifiers: LCCN 2024018204 | ISBN 9798990014954 (trade paperback)
Subjects: LCGFT: Novels.
Classification: LCC PS3601.L4149 M36 2024 | DDC 813/.6--dc23/eng/20240503
LC record available at https://lccn.loc.gov/2024018204

Cover art: Gronk, *Untitled*, mixed media on paper, 2023
Book design by Ash Good, www.ashgood.com

What Books Press
363 South Topanga Canyon Boulevard
Topanga, CA 90290

WHATBOOKSPRESS.COM

I am resolved, only towards what I don't know.
—Student

You've no idea what a pile of things I have to tell you.
—Walser

Why don't you pull yourself to pieces!
—Marx

THE MANUSCRIPTS

I JUST WANTED to ask my question, my question that was about the hat. But the question about the hat would have to wait. Indeed, the wife of the Philosopher was asking me to wait, there on the telephone. I could hear her, the telephone receiver surely tucked against her bosom, and through the muffle of her telephonic embrace I heard her call his name, his name which I omit here at the behest of the Driver (whom I will discuss in the pages to come).

When the Philosopher came to the telephone, he did not bring it up to his face, but rather he and his wife engaged in a discussion—a discussion of who was calling on him. My ears were tucked there in the receiver (which now, I imagined, was clutched between them like the forty-five a goon trains discreetly on the midsection of a pulp-fiction protagonist), and the discussion the Philosopher and his wife engaged in volleyed the topic of the caller (myself, the chronicler of these pages) and my intentions (as yet unstated to the Philosopher's wife, though not to you). In the way the Philosopher responded to everything his wife said—that is, with the fishhooks of unanswerable questions—I heard the tenacious and even pugnacious approach to discourse for which he had come to be known, though soon the tight dialectic spiraled into other questions of: Were the onions burning, and if so was it butter or lard in which they'd been softening on the stove, and where had she found this lard, what with the shortages and the rations? And she demurred, and by the time she finally admitted that she'd gotten a grip of lard from the man who'd recently taken up occupancy in the gray house down the road, for which she'd promised him some mending, I realized that the telephone receiver that was my proxy into this domestic scene had been set atop the table, and that the man in the gray house did not have the complete approval of the Philosopher, as the man in the gray house was new to this road, and thus could not be trusted. The Philosopher's wife brought up the point that the new man in the gray house was now trusted because he had exchanged the good of this lard for the service of her mending, that trust was a product of social exchange, not a precondition for it. This seemed to rattle the Philosopher, as his response took the form of a scribble: jagged sentences interrupted by the beginnings of new sentences heading in new directions, which were in turn interrupted, and so forth. (Knowing the Philosopher's predilection for geometric representations of thought and its articulations—you will recall the Vorticist illustrations he himself drew for the Imperative appendix—this description feels apt.)

Once things had settled between the two, the dinner seemed, or sounded, quite nice, and their discussion turned to the weather (bad) and what it foretold (bad things), then to the vicissitudes of typewriters (it seemed that the Philosopher's wife was typing up some missives from his hand-written drafts, informing him about some emendations she had made), and while he was informing her that the problem was not so much the regular breakdowns of typewriting machines but rather that the effort of repair shackled people to be the maintainers of the technology rather than the beneficiaries of its so-called advances, she was explaining how in his letter to the new rector of the university she thought it better to begin with a softer tone, inquiring, say, about the well-being of his family, before introducing the nature of his query in the second paragraph.

—It shows you're human, she said.

—They're lethal, he said, these machines.

It certainly was thrilling, to share such an intimate meal with the Philosopher's family of two (a number already halved by the war), as I myself was, with the receiver shouldered to my ear, spooning potato soup drippingly into my mouth. Naturally, I wished I could be sharing the meal that the Philosopher and his wife were sharing—and what was it, something with onion, of course, perhaps with a mirepoix base (the three of us, we slurped in synchronicity)—but I found an odd comfort in this arrangement, something akin to the forms of sociability that the Philosopher himself said occur in places spatially and temporally distinct that are mediated by art, those spaces like the facets of a diamond, both fractured and creating a whole.

It was nice, our meal. Outside the window—that is, outside my window, or rather my aunt's window—the moon was visible in diaphanous loungewear, where it had previously been completely obscured, and I wondered if its late appearance might be noticed by my dinnermates and if so what they might make of it, if they might amend their earlier premonitions, but they were now cleaning up, which was a silent affair, though not really silent: The sonar blips of prandial objects, the clink of utensil, the ceramic scrape of plate, they choreographed a dumbshow of domestic routine, and I took the opportunity to likewise place my bowl in the cluttered clay basin of my aunt's sink. The telephone receiver still tucked against my ear, the sounds of my little kitchen tasks momentarily covered the sound of someone picking up the other telephone receiver. The Philosopher said into my ear,

—Is someone there?

And I was struck silent. The direct address, like a movie actor turning to the camera and finding my eyes alone in a darkened theater, it was alienating in its sudden intimacy. He said,

—Hello?

I gathered my thoughts, realigned them with my fine motor skills, and I spoke. I introduced myself, reported to him that I was a student and a great reader of his, and I explained that I was housed nearby for the time being, having recently arrived from F—— to assist my aunt in her dotage, a duty for which I was hiating my final year of university. I did not mention how my taking up residency here was motivated in part by the proximity it offered to the Philosopher himself and the answers he surely possessed about the hat; instead, I told him how surprised and delighted I'd been to hear that I was now his neighbor, as I was a great reader of his work, and that I had a most important question. The Philosopher, his voice tickling

11

the hairs in my ears as if he were perched small on my shoulder, my own personal Philosopher, said,

—Not interested.

And he ended the telephone connection.

It was three days later that we reconnected, though by way of a different medium, and during that time I chopped, per my aunt's request, one cord of wood, storing the lumber neatly in the shed where it would stay dry. There were other chores, but the wood chopping is the activity that now seems to measure that time, as the rhythm of it, both in body and object, was gratifying for the ways it aligned the corporeal and the temporal. Each log had approximately the diameter of my torso, and when I hefted one I had to hug it with both arms. With a section of log propped upright before me, I examined the plate-size cross-section of tree, its fingerprint rings, sliding my dominant hand up to the smooth hilt of the axe, keeping my non-dominant hand at the base of the handle, that wood smoothed by countless hands, that slow attrition forming a contrast to the quick splitting action of the axe blade, contrasting both in action and in time. My lungs filled as the axe rose, held captive my breath as I brought the axe down, and poofed out in the snap of impact. For long stretches of unmeasurable time, which might not be time at all, the axe remained completely outside my visual range. It was not something I was consciously aware of; it was an extension of my body, less an object in action than an object as action. The sound of its blade splitting one log into two was like a simple, satisfying bite into a crisp apple. I arranged each half of the freshly split log, and in two hits I quartered them. I could, theoretically, keep halving each log and never run out of log, the infinite hiding in division not multiplication, but I stopped at turning each length of log into four. In the dirt, the mud, surrounding me, and my multiplying, shrinking logs, which were protected from the dampness of the ground by a thick sheet of canvas, which I would soon fold up and haul into the shed, I noticed that the clumpy consistency atop the loamy, liquidy soil resembled that in *A Straw Hat*.

That's the painting that had been the subject of my question, my question being the occasion for my telephone call to the Philosopher's house. But it is not quite right to say that it was just the painting that was the subject of the question; my question was also about the hat itself, its owner and wearer, and the Philosopher's explication of it all in his monograph on aesthetics, which had been brought to my attention way back in my first year of university.

I had been spending much of my time on studies of a composition of my grandfather, whom I had never met. He was a tiller in the north of M——, but he did not live to see its devastation, and when people spoke of him they spoke of him as an avatar of antebellum bliss, pastoral and sublime, man and earth in concert—specifically, Grandpa and earth. The particulars of his demise were unknown, and now that most all of his progeny had been eradicated by two conflicts and the flu and famine of the interbella, save myself and my aunt, I had become, upon my entrance into university, compelled to preserve what I knew of him in the only medium I felt I could control with any adroitness: charcoal, graphite, any mineral scraped against thick pulpy paper, the abrasion of elements. And as my compositions became less focused on the face that I never saw, they became more detailed in the detail that I knew: He wore a hat, a straw hat. And my knowledge of this hat was not just from my knowledge of the Platonic general (hat *qua* hat), but rather an encounter with the specific artifact, the particular, instantiate hat of my grandfather. It had hung—straw crumbling, but still holding enough of its structural integrity to be called a hat—in my aunt's home, in her closet.

That was one reason for my journey back to this region, this darkly fecund region that was not mine by birth, but mine by looming obligation, tucked into a country through which travel, in these months after the final cessation of the violence, was quite inconvenient, even for an unaffiliated student like myself. But, regarding the hat and my studies of it, it was in my first year at university, as my renderings of this hat were becoming more intricate and precise, those straws giving a phantom bristle against the skin upon glimpse of its graphite likeness, that a professor mentioned to me the Philosopher's monograph *Towards a Complete Aesthetics*, in which he explicated another hat, and I was compelled to wonder if we might have been considering the same hat.

The subject of *Towards a Complete Aesthetics* is the famous oil painting *A Straw Hat* (19—), about which the Philosopher demonstrates his method of heuristic direct description. His ekphrastic meditation on the painting of the hat includes not just the thing itself—"the thing's thingliness"—but sly slices of information on the Artist's means of creating this work: namely that at the time he had been staying in the north of M——. The Philosopher spends a good paragraph detailing what kind of life the details of this dirty, ground-strewn straw hat reveal about the wearer: "The farmer wears the hat in the field. Only there is it what it is. Equipmentally, it is a shield of the sun, a caul between man and nature: a technology. And yet, the more the hat is itself in-being, the less the farmer is aware of it. The farmer, meanwhile, only becomes aware of the hat, not when it is in-being upon his head, but when it falls to the ground, as it is here, returning to the earth as pure potentiality. And yet, it is only in the painting that we notice these things, both the hat and the animating attention of the wearer. And yet—."

(I supply this passage not from an open book but from my memory, which is quite good, as I do not have access to the Philosopher's *Towards a Complete Aesthetics* in the attic in which I write this.)

It is well within the parameters of reason for me to suggest that this hat was my grandfather's. The Artist was staying in the north of M——, where in 19— my grandfather was working as a tiller. I have seen the famous oil painting (a reproduction of it), and the hat it depicts greatly resembles the hat that presently rests on a hook in my aunt's closet (or rather it greatly resembles a more complete earlier form of the hat, its brim more a Saturn's ring than its current thorny crown). And yet, it is not the painting that most interests me (even though I am a student of the visual arts), nor is it the Artist whose audience I sought (he died of consumption somewhere in Q——). Rather, it was the Philosopher's evocation of my grandfather that I was most drawn to, the Philosopher whose audience I needed. I needed to know all that might be concealed in the aposiopesis of that final "And yet—." Where might that sentence have gone? Like a plank off the starboard side of one of Robert Louis Stevenson's pirate ships, that em-dash drops us off into a dark ocean of the unknown, though perhaps not the unknowable, as the Philosopher was clearly drawing on some uncited knowledge of the Artist's means of creation. And so: Did the Artist meet my grandfather? Did they know each other? What did the Artist learn of my grandfather, and what did the Philosopher know of any of this? Had my grandfather perished in the war, that other war, the previous one? These were the questions swimming like opalescent guppies beneath the surface of a calm pond as I called on the Philosopher that night (I'm sure my voice on the telephone was calm: clear and confident). And those were the questions that continued their soft but incessant wriggling as I went about my other duties: There was the cistern, which needed to be filled from the well; there was the clearing out of my cousins' rooms, hauling out the familystuffs not needed for nostalgia; there were the boxes of documents that needed to be taken to the incinerator, and all the other chores, none of which I found as aesthetically satisfying as the wood-chopping.

Perhaps the least aesthetically satisfying chore, however, was changing out my aunt's bedpan. She was less and less ambulatory and had recently invested in a replacement horn for a gramophone, arrived by post, which she did not use on a gramophone (she did not have one); rather, she would place the small end to her mouth, direct the flowering end up into the air, and call to me, the simple if ornate device amplifying her imperatives not only across the house but beyond into the unplowed acreage, turning the heads of all the bad farmers in the land. This loamy, lime-rich corner of a clay-dense country attracted tuberous people who somehow, despite their reveries about soil, could extract nothing but stone and old tire scraps from its dirty bosom. The Philosopher often referred to this province as prelapsarian and yet most here seemed less pre-something and more post-something, seeming to have fled, long before the war and its compulsories, an awful unnamed something, retreated here where no one discussed the nature of your being here much less the nature of Being (the renown of the Philosopher, I had found out as I inquired about him to neighbors, was largely unknown).

Regardless, my aunt's investment in this detached gramophone horn seemed to be a tacit admission (prediction) that she had no plans to leave her bed anymore, just as my agreeing to take one year off university to assist her in the upkeep of her estate was a tacit admission (prediction) that she would, by the year's end, no longer need the assistance of anyone other than an undertaker. The changing of the bedpan was not an edifying experience, and yet my aunt always attempted to turn it into one. She took my momentary audience as an opportunity to expound on a great number of subjects, today's being the troubled future of our lineage.

We were, it seemed, the last of us. On her bedroom walls existed everyone who'd ceased to exist, framed in five-by-eight sepia. With gestures that left the objects of her vaguely pronounced stories a bit unclear, she discussed the problems of a family ill-equipped to multiply. Though my distaff line was more spirited, my spear line, it seemed, was onanistic temperamentally, propagating incidentally. It is said (by her) that I might be the only human to be the product of three generations of virgin birth. (And if the effect of coition was achieved so regularly without any actual coition, then it raises the question of what coition actually is!) My great-grandfather, a garment worker, offered himself a storage-room release into the silky crotchal sling of a pair of women's unmentionables that somehow incubated the milt until a woman wore them and found herself unbleeding and sore-breasted, a woman who traced the incident back to the garment worker and made sure she didn't birth a bastard, a (barely) non-bastard who grew up and grew into the affections of ginger-locked, freckle-sprayed woman who sensed a skittishness in the young man who had clearly tilled nothing more than shit-clotted earth (this was he of the straw hat) and so lured him into a warm bath only for him to see, upon her easing herself into the same bath, the milky smoke-curls about him in the water, which surely swam her way, as the lack of consummation from a geometrical standpoint, of shapes fitting inside shapes, held no bearing on the evidence of consummation soon growing, that evidence being my father, who, in a health screening during a stay at a sanitarium, produced vials of fluids for inspection, said vials then being grossly misappropriated by staff who also treated my aunt's sister in a different wing of the sanitarium, who became my mother before ever meeting my father, though the staff, for all their faults, did make sure to compel these two into matrimony once the result of their little experiment (hello!) emerged. (I should note that all these people are now dead.) So, my aunt was explaining, as my gaze moved forlornly over the faces of these men and women, eyes shadowed, cheeks sallow, postures rigidly bent, this was a problem—a problem that eventually fell on the progeny, of which I was the only one worth a fuck. (That was how she put it. Her diction was of the country, just as salty as the well water.) Though we weren't royalty and a lack of a lineage, a scion getting snipped off, did not pose problems of political instability and internecine tribal conflict, the family dying with me did present existential conundrums I was not daft to, though I had no immediate solution to the problem. My aunt, however, did have a solution. She said,

—Screw. Like a priapic fiend. Like your name depends on it, because it does. After all, what use is a tool if you don't use it?

I briefly became excited to explain to her what the Philosopher had written about a tool's unreadiness-at-hand, but in the moment it took me to gather my thoughts, my aunt had continued onto a different subclaim: that I should not waste myself in art. Art was onanistic by definition, and doom by extension.

No, she insisted, I needed to get into politics, which, she insisted, was much more fucky. That was the sphere, she said, where I could put my tool to good use. But, I explained, the apolitical nature of art is precisely what makes it a system of meaning-making that moves toward Truth; it is predicated on the I, which is why it is authentic, whereas the political is a system of meaning-making that moves away from Truth; it is predicated on the Them, which is why it is inauthentic. Besides, I explained, it was inauthenticity that got people killed.

That must have been when the letter arrived. I should note that my aunt's house did not normally receive post. This was a product both of temperament and cartography: To the former, she despised people knocking on her door, snooping onto her her property, especially people in uniform, the colors of which were not always clear in our smeary rural haze; after she injured the third postman—she still had her crossbow—the postmaster proposed that she come pick up her own deliveries (pickupperies) at their office once a week. To the latter, her address was not something that most postmen had been trained to decipher, as it was not the typical code of plot and path, region and route, that made most envelope-fronts appear equation-like in their dense numberiness; rather, her address appeared more descriptive than coded, formatted as a complete paragraph, explaining in layman syntax the location of her house, coordinating its location against natural and easily recognizable landmarks. This system of address was at violent odds with the standards of the postmaster, but it seems to have been a vestigial scrap of wayfinding that somehow managed to survive the long-ago Unification effort, of which the standardization of addresses was a major part, and yet my maternal grandmother seemed to have fought valiantly to maintain this arcane address and here I was, well into the twentieth century, staying in a house without a number.

Which is to say, we—the postman clutching an envelope, and I holding open the front door, while my aunt, upstairs, announced via gramophone horn that her tray of sugarcubes was empty—were both a bit confused to be facing each other, that single envelope, bearing a blank face, no name or block of exposition on its front, held between us. I took the envelope, started to ask how he found—when he interrupted to say that the man down the road in the thatch-roof number (this was the Philosopher's house) had flagged him down and given him a brick-hard loaf of bread as payment to deliver this directly to this home. So I took the envelope, grateful that my aunt no longer had the upper body strength to nock her crossbow, if she'd even seen this man approach, then I closed the door. I granted myself permission to, with the dispassion of a caretaker whose purview must extend to issues of post, open the unaddressed envelope. This might have seemed a greater violation of my aunt's privacy had we not once lived under the watchful eye of the now-deposed administration's censors who read postal correspondence with care, leaving no trace save for the occasional tear-smeared word on passages of sorrow (only once did a letter arrive to my university dormitory from my mother—her final before her passing—that was atangle with doodles like an illuminated manuscript, the margins depicting the sequential adventures of a lone man—an avatar, I suspected, of the bored bureaucrat whose desk this passed over—whose body was composed of stickly lines save for his increasingly and alarmingly growing phallus; the narrative that clotted my mother's letter, which was otherwise informing me about the selling of my childhood belongings, seemed to be a quest, a quest to find somewhere to put such a monstrous appendage; war had turned everyone amorous).

So I did open the envelope only to find—beneath the stationary banner blaring the extravagantly seriffed name of the Philosopher—that the letter was addressed to: me. Had I told him, in our brief exchange on the telephone, my name? Yes, I must have. Or at least I told his wife, and since this letter was typed, it meant that it had passed under the editorial eye of the Philosopher's wife. Beyond my name, beyond the vocative comma tucked under the last letter like a simple house slipper, was a block of text I dared not read. For reasons I could not parse, the jolt of adrenaline that squirted through my brain upon seeing that the Philosopher had actually addressed a communication to me caused me to immediately tear the letter in half, then into quarters, mimicking the same division of a neatly split log. I looked at the scraps of paper and I screamed in a spike of countertenor. What had I done? And why had I done? I held the scraps of the letter in my hand and rushed up to my aunt's room, where she sat upright in bed holding her little green tray as if in hollow oblation: It bore no sugarcubes and, worse, I was bringing her not a refill but the traces of my letter and panic-serrated pleas for her to help me piece it back together. I sat on her bed and spread the pieces over the quilt between us, fitting them together like a puzzle. I found *to eagerly have you as a guest* and, noting the characteristic use of a split infinitive, a common tic/flourish of his prose, waved the thumb-size piece of paper before my aunt, who was asking,

—Do they have a daughter or two that you could bed?

I aligned the deckle-edge of that scrap with one that mentioned *the possibility of engaging you for some travel*, and, as I yelped with glee, realized that such prose stylings might actually have been—this whole time—that of his wife the typist and covert copyeditor, while my aunt was saying,

—Travel will be good, plenty ripe cunny out there, as long as you don't go around saying you're an artist.

And as part of my brain was occupied disaggregating all the possibilities of the Philosopher's wife's influence on the texts that I had for years now taken as a single ecstatic burst of a single consciousness, I fit in another piece of the letter with *the caveat of your unaffiliated status*, and of course I had remained unaffiliated, would not have been able to travel across regional borders had I been otherwise, would not have been able to come back here to tend to my aunt who was now gesturing, her forearm as phallus, all that I should do to those, in her words, nubile vamps who hung out in the neighboring district. My aunt—who seemed to have me mistaken for that cartoon penis-man doodled on my mother's letter all that time ago—had more precise advice for activities, which I omit here, except to say I have since, in my travels with the Philosopher, attempted one such activity and it did not work in the slightest.

—I'm to be a dinner guest at their house, I told my aunt. For real this time.

Arranging such appointments could be a confusing affair, so I decided to head straight over. For the occasion, my aunt insisted that I dress in the suit my uncle had been buried in because, she said, he could blast a tunnel through the Alps.

—But I thought his trade was haberdashery, I said.

She just told me to focus on my buttons. And she was right; it was a buttonsome garment that required my full attention. My aunt confirmed the proper alignment of my placket, warning me not to attempt to use the pockets because she made a habit of sewing up the pockets of the dead with earthly tokens, and she saw me out.

I walked the short distance to the Philosopher's house—I'm not much for measuring spatial distance beyond the eleven-by-fourteen inches of a piece of drafting paper, more inclined to measuring temporal distance, so I remember the distance between the two houses as being the length it took me to thricely sing to myself "I Can't Begin To Tell You" by Bing Crosby—and just as the anxiety of having to knock on the Philosopher's front door began to grip me, I saw that there wouldn't be the need to present myself: The Philosopher's wife was tending to the shrubbery and had already seen me approaching. She wore dungarees and a cable-knit sweater. When I neared the shin-high rock wall that perimetered their property, she said,

—Thought a dead man was dropping by for a visit.

I explained that it wasn't me, it was my suit, that my uncle had—

—I know who that suit belongs to, she said. And that means I know who you are.

She waved me closer, past the rock wall, kept waving me with both hands—like she was on a runway guiding a biplane to takeoff—into the house in which my eyes took longer than expected to dilate to the unlit space, the space that revealed itself to be occupied largely by a long table that on one end seemed to serve the purposes of the kitchen (the gashes and gouges of cooking implements in the unfinished maple) and on the other end the administrative tasks of a household (small stacks of paper, their trifolds suggesting they came by post, weighed down with chess pieces). The Philosopher's wife said,

—We are about to have our meal. You will stay.

I sat midway down the long table, warmed by both the cindering hearth and the offer of mealtime fellowship, and while I was distracted by trying to see, across the dim room, just what she was preparing, the Philosopher materialized.

Here he was beside me, and I beside him. His hereness, then, was contingent upon me and mine his. He was a bit taller than I'd imagined, though the low ceiling of his living room might have added a few illusory inches to his stooped frame. Furrows on his brow seemed to be in the slow act of sweeping away the dust of his eyebrows, below which a bulbous nose sprouted a pyramidal mustache that had remained strikingly dark while the rest had gone a ghostly gray. He said hello and mumbled,

—I normally sit here,

He took a spot just to my right, but in a moment—during which I remained silent—he appeared discomfited and stood back up and walked around to the other side of the table where he took a seat across from me.

—This will have to do.

My fingers were finding the grooves and knots in the tabletop. My uncle's suit had found the split in my backside and seemed determined to elongate it a few inches. He was a thirty-eight regular, I a thirty-eight tall. My silence seemed to have the effect of trapped steam. The Philosopher said, simply,

—So.

And that was the flick that opened the valve, and suddenly I was talking, talking about who I was and who he was, as if he needed an introduction to himself and his work, and about how much his work had meant to me, as an artist, as a thinker, as a being in the world, and as someone simply trying to answer a few questions about where I came from.

—You see, I continued, in *Aesthetics* there is the matter of the straw hat, of the tiller who must have worn that hat—

But I was interrupted when his wife delivered the meal to the table: two plates that carried nothing but a single blood sausage each. I knew that dish from both sight and rusted smell. It was not an uncommon serving in our house during periods of economic uncertainty, and I associate the taste with dread. I was a little taken aback at it being on the (formidable) table of the great Philosopher, as it is very much the cuisine of the peasantry, and until quite recently he had held the eminent rectorship of his university. But of course I recalled the rapturous ways he'd written about the lifestyle of the earth-worker, and how skeptical he'd been about the impulse of urban cuisine toward aggregation. I made a mental note not to ask for a cognac as a digestif after the meal, but then I realized I did not have a meal. As the Philosopher and his wife each tended to their scabby defecate, I stared down at my absence of a plate. She had said that we were about to eat, and sure enough the clusivity of that pronoun was devious. I was relieved to not have a blood sausage in front of me and also madly desirous of one. The Philosopher said,

—I have requested you here because you have recently traveled across regional borders. I am allowed no such privilege, as I have been marked Class Four.

This revelation was punctuated by his wife slapping the table in anger.

—You surely know this. I am—stuck here, for the time being, rooted like a damn tree.

—Rooted, I said, like what you've written about the aesthetic object being by necessity rooted.

—Yes, he said, well, that's—

—And, I continued, only when the aesthetic object is rooted and fixed in temporality, in both the subject of the hat and the material creation of the paint that renders the hat, can we recognize our own subject position, and—

—That's all well and good, my boy, but—

—That's when we care. That's when we cathect with the aesthetic object, and that's the path to unconcealment. Sir, this hat, I need to know something about it.

I appeared to be holding a fork that did not belong to me. Its tines bore jiggling bits of black sausage. I apologized to the Philosopher's wife and replaced the utensil to her plateside. She nodded kindly. The Philosopher cupped his warm hand over mine. Now his hand was over mine, mine under his. His nowness, then, was contingent upon me and mine his. He shushed, the bristles of his mustache rustling.

—You are excitable, he said. I like that. We need excitement. I assure you, my boy, I will do my best to answer all your questions. But first, I must ask you for something.

He patted my forearm, then leaned back. The sweat his meaty paw had left on the back of my hand made my skin slightly cool. The Philosopher said to me,

—I am interested in acquiring your assistance for a bit of travel. You see, as the situation here was getting more and more troublesome, I took some of my papers and I kept them with associates in neighboring regions. For safekeeping. These papers comprise three lengthy chapters that have been the focus of all my intellectual energy these recent years. I couldn't risk storing it wholly in one place, vulnerable to confiscation, so I divided the three chapters into the homes of three different associates. Well, things have now turned, haven't they. I need to retrieve those manuscripts. It's time I finish this. It's been over twenty years. But as a Class Four, I am unable to cross regional borders.

He slouched lower over his empty plate. He appeared like an animal whose body was starting to distort to the confines of his cage; and as his movement was circumscribed, so too was that of his mind, as its work was now alienated from him. My fingers manipulated the jacket pocket that my aunt had sewn shut; through the cloth, I could feel the dim contours of an object, small and flat, that would remain unknown to me.

—At least not until we get that sorted out, the Philosopher continued. It's just bureaucracy, you see. But it can take a long time to get it straight.

So: You will smuggle me across those borders, and then smuggle me, and my manuscripts, back.

I did not have an automobile. But I would not worry about that yet. I knew what those papers were. I knew what it had been *over twenty years* since. He was talking about the long-awaited Part Two to the Part One that had been published in the droughty, dreary year of my birth. Although some say the book is impossible to read, it's impossible rather to understate its accomplishments. It finally discovered the possibilities and parameters of human actuality, from the experience of a splinter to the experience of a soul. But more than that: In giving us the tools to grasp our existence the book had forever altered the very existence we were finally grasping. While millennia of philosophers had theorized about why the moon, the Philosopher reminded the world that the moon was "the moon" because it was seen and comprehended and questioned by *us*. The world was not just objects; it was objects in relation to subjects, experiencing subjects experiencing subjectivity through objects, as we were "human beings who were entities which in our Being have this very Being as an issue." It was the book that—reading through the Philosopher's entire extant corpus in the months after that professor had first drawn my attention to *Aesthetics* and its hat—made me pause midpage, look up from a bus stop in a city increasingly hollowed out by a violence I didn't understand, and say aloud that I am a person in the world, that recognition plucking at the meniscus of my very ontology.

I recalled that hollowed-out scenery again when I went looking for a bustling city center within walking distance of my aunt's house, finding instead boarded-up windows. I was now attempting to solve the problem of not having an automobile, and my solution seemed simple: I'd post a driver-wanted sign and pay this driver half of the recompense the Philosopher had offered me for labor and hardship. And of course I'd accepted the Philosopher's assignment. I'd accepted it with stuttering, weepy zeal. Having a vital role to play in ushering Part Two of his magnum opus into the world was an honor too great for my consciousness to fully grasp: an experience that defines the sublime. While in Part One he'd grappled with the rootedness and historical contingency of Being, Part Two promised to solve the great problems of rootlessness and the supratemporalicity of the unworlded, and now I would be, if only briefly, custodian to those manuscripts. And the Philosopher had been right: It was *time* he finished it. The world had been ruptured and Part Two promised repair.

As I searched storefronts for posted bills, hoping to find local help-wanted postings and finding only missing persons queries, a roster of have-you-seens, I considered what this place had looked like five, ten years earlier, a century earlier. All I could imagine was a multiplicity of my grandfather, everyone wearing the same muddied straw hat.

On a bare patch of wood that seemed to have hosted an assortment of postings the meaning and function of which remained opaque to me, I placed the post I had prepared. In direct language, it requested transportation in an automobile that had the space in its trunk to hold the body of at least one full-grown human male. The post also mentioned modest compensation. With the palm of my left hand, I steadied the paper against the wood, holding a small picture-frame nail in my fingers, while with my right hand I raised the ball-peen hammer and—as the hammer left my field of vision, left the realm of my conscious awareness and become a ready-at-hand extension of my body, even while I thrilled at the realization that I was experiencing the very extra-conscious, embodied *toolness* that the Philosopher had so elegantly articulated—brought it down on the delicate-looking nailhead.

I immediately heard a loud bark from inside this building. I stumbled back, satisfied to see that in only one hammer-strike, my post had stuck true to the place at which I had stuck it—which turned out to be a door that presently swung open, revealing a very round and very angry-looking man. He looked at what I'd left on his door and said,

—Hey, Martin Luther! What's this bullshit?

Just as his suspenders held his trousers from falling to his ankles, his sideburns seemed to keep his jaw cinched tight to his face, words escaping through the very tight egress of a lipless mouth. Sideburns with no mustache or beard was a choice men of this or any region did not much make. I, my feet striking a stance that had me ready to retreat if need be, explained my mission. The man (whose undershirt was not underneath anything, was in fact exposed in all its soup-stained expressionism to the world) said,

—Yes, I can see that. You just repeated verbatim what it says here.

He tore my post from its nail, waved it. His fingers had the dirt-darkened nailbeds of the kind of craftsmen that populated the Philosopher's writings, in their workshops, in the world. I elaborated. I explained with full transparency. The Philosopher needed my help in retrieving his manuscripts, and because of the new regulations and confounded classifications he was unable to cross regional borders to do so. I needed an automobile to help him. When I began explaining the thrust and force of the Philosopher's writings, in order to give some idea of what a trove of revelations these new manuscripts might hold for us, and the world, this man interrupted to say,

—This says here compensation. How much?

I told him, explaining that while the Philosopher's former rectorship was a position of great status it was not of great salary. The man's hairline mouth puckered inward in thought. He nodded swiftly but erratically, as if shaking a gnat from his nose.

—I will do it.

—What?

—We will use my vehicle. We leave tonight?

Flummoxed, I fixated on the fine print. What of the trunk space? When crossing the borders we needed to obscure our very important passenger.

—It's a two-body trunk, he said. Trust me. No problem.

He handed me my posting and told me to write down where he should rendezvous with me and the Philosopher for the starting of our journey. Not having the Philosopher's exact address in my head, I began writing down my aunt's phenomenological address.

And so it seemed this simple quest would satisfy all: I would get an intimate audience with the Philosopher who held the answer to my hat question; the Philosopher would regain possession of his manuscripts; my aunt would see me venture off to sew my wild oats; and as for the Driver, I didn't know much about him and his goals at this point, but he seemed happy for the money. All would be perfect!

All is quite crummy in this attic. Crummy in the sense of the biscuit crumbs I can't seem to keep corralled to the plate I have beside this typewriter, and crummy in the sense of how the ceiling lets in a finger-numbing chill. I keep hearing movement in the house below and thinking it might be the Driver, or his Compeer, but it is almost certainly the crepitation of this old house in the wind, its joints arthritic. The window over the cot—I have stood up and looked out many times to try and see the detached garage, but I cannot see it. No matter how I smoosh my face to the glass, the arrangement of structures remains rigid, noncompliant to my desire to just glimpse where the Philosopher is now captive. Whenever I walk between my little typewriter table here and the window, my footsteps send the floorboards complaining, and I worry about waking the Driver and the Compeer, if they are indeed sleeping. If I am unable to rest tonight, I at least want to reduce myself to the sound of sleep. Nothing but the clacking typewriter to check off the seconds until sunrise. Sunrise, and then what? I do not want to return to my aunt. I do not want to return to my studies. I want to know what I want. The gas lamp beside me flickers when troubled by the draft, though tracking the source of the draft, the exact fissure between floorboards or wallboards or ceilingboards, has proven impossible. My investigations into the ceilingboards, though—standing on this wobbly chair to raise my head through the rafters and closer to the canted ceiling—has attuned me to the tiny footsteps up there. I cannot imagine what kind of rodent might be keeping sentry on the roof. It is surely too high a summit for a racoon or squirrel or skunk. Whatever species is patrolling the stately crenelations of the Compeer's incongruous house, I hope it is one that will not try to infiltrate my little attic. I have had my fill this evening of hectic runnings-around. I need rest, rest that will not come. I need resolution, resolution that will not come.

The best I can hope for is putting one word after another. If Being precedes thought, but only thought can disclose Being, then I can create here a site of unconcealment, a site built by language. This seems to me impossible, to disclose the thing that precedes language by ensnaring it with language. Maybe it's just a matter of velocity. The velocity of language. If I put one word after another fast enough, velocity increasing exponentially, then eventually I will reach this very moment: Being will be disclosed; I will have successfully tracked all causal chains to this moment; I will feel the release of exculpation. And if I can write through the past and into the present, then there is no reason that I cannot write the future (at least according to the laws of physics, one should be able to remember the future as one remembers the past; or at least according to a bespectacled physics student who, breath minty with anise, once told me that), writing into a future in which my part in this will feel like a thing resolved. The addressee, then, of this *to whom it may concern* (hello, whomever!) is a me that just isn't yet.

The Driver arrived at my aunt's house at sundown. His automobile was not the small bubbly thing of the average motorist, nor was it the flatbed I would have imagined a gentleman of the earth like the Driver to operate; it was a sedan, a large one, with a front-end that announced its presence with a regal aggression. The paint job was freckled with rust, but it was otherwise in alarmingly good condition. The Driver remained at the wheel, gave the horn a small toot, and waited, staring resolutely ahead. I watched this from the window of my aunt's bedroom, where, after she'd mended my clothes for the journey, I'd readied her for sleep: a tincture of chloral hydrate, a kiss on the forehead. I told her I'd be home by sun-up. Her eyelids starting to droop, she held my wrist and said,

—Take a flower from the linden tree out by the toolshed. The flower is a soft little burst of yellow and it smells invitingly of honey and lemon. Take one of these flowers, rub its stamen between your fingers, and touch the pollen behind your scrotum.

She smiled. The linden tree had been dead since my arrival.

—The women will appreciate it.

And as Hypnos carried her off, I carried myself down the stairs and out the door, and when I approached the formidable machine, I patted its roof and said,

—Ahoy, Argo!

I got into the back seat, saving the passenger seat for our esteemed passenger, and continued:

—And that makes you Jason, and me the crew of Argonauts.

The Driver, keeping his eyes on the dark road ahead, told me that his name was not Jason.

—Yes, of course, I said, but the Golden Fleece! Retrieved by Jason and the Argonauts, vesseled along to Colchis in the sturdy ship, the Argo.

The Driver asked for directions to the Philosopher's house. After I directed him, I said,

—I suppose I could be the Jason, if that's not too presumptuous of me. Or no, of course—what am I thinking?—we are about to pick up our Jason, right up here on the left, in fact.

There, silhouetted in the road, was the Philosopher. He had on a hat. I regretted my uncovered head. He also held a suitcase. I became concerned that I'd misheard his assurance that this would just be the work of one night, that the safehouses-cum-archives on our agenda were, though separated by regional borders, within a night's motoring distance. Once the Driver came to a stop— the slowing crunch of gravel, the squeak of the clutch and break—I opened the door and walked around to take the suitcase from the Philosopher. Expecting a great weight, I wound up jerking the portmanteau up above my shoulders. The Philosopher said,

—You're stronger than you realize.

I puffed with pride. As he let himself into the passenger seat of the sedan, I took the suitcase into the back seat with me and, upon realizing that he'd brought it to carry his manuscripts home, my pride revealed itself to be as empty as the bag. I tapped my fingers on the suitcase's rigid leather, enjoyed the hollow thump in counterpoint to the rumble of tires on tank-shredded road.

As the glow of the Philosopher's house dimmed to a flicker behind us, I introduced the two men. I watched them nod silent acknowledgment at each other, and I became anxious for them to find fast and easy concord, as if I were introducing two of my oldest and dearest friends. The headlamps of the Driver's automobile caught little clouds of buglife. The road was now textured more by cartwheels and hooves than by whitewalls and Goodyears. Around us, pine and spruce proliferated, becoming increasingly dense as we progressed toward the border, unless tree density was an illusion created by the Driver increasing our speed. The vibrations on my backside suggested the latter. As if continuing a conversation we'd already been long enjoying, I said,

—So, this flora is not dissimilar to that found in the north of M———. You will recall, sir, that is where *A Straw Hat* was composed. As I believe I mentioned to you, my grandfather worked as a tiller in the north of M———.

I paused to investigate the shadowy nape of the Philosopher, hoping it might show the tendon-tightening of recognition. I saw nothing but an untidy neckline. I turned to the Driver, my change in address more tonal than anything, in the hopes that offering him some exposition might indirectly prompt the Philosopher to begin filling in the needed details on the painting and my forefather. I said,

—Are you familiar with our passenger's great monograph *Towards a Complete Aesthetics*? It's quite remarkable. In fact, it entirely redesigned my thinking about my craft. You see, I'm an artist. My medium is visual, though I am flattered that our esteemed passenger taxonomizes the visual arts alongside the poetic. At this particular moment in my apprenticeship, I mostly do charcoal still lifes, vanitas. I hope to expand into other media, though the war has created a great dearth of materials, like canvas and certain pigments like Prussian blue, as well as a great dearth of mentoring artists at my university. The sculptors are all quite dead, for example. Regardless—

The Driver pulled over to the side of the road. He pointed into the dark and said the first border was half a kilometer ahead. As the Philosopher opened his door and got out, I said,

—Oh, I imagined that we'd have a little more driving time than that, but that's okay—that's great, in fact! Fleet to the Golden Fleece!

As the Driver removed himself from the automobile, too, I was struck by how silently they moved to their tasks: Neither had needed to verbally outline what he or the other was to do; they simply did it. The Driver was already opening the trunk. I got out and did my best to assist the Philosopher into the trunk. The Driver had perhaps been exaggerating, as we all do when employment is on offer, to say that this was a two-body trunk; it was more like a Philosopher and a half in capacity, but regardless it would do the trick. With the Philosopher tucked fetally into the trunk, I asked if I should put the suitcase in there as well, but the Philosopher—the cramping of lungs audible in the suddenly nasal quality of his voice—said we would worry about that after it had his papers in it. Staring ahead at the black metal interior of the trunk, the Philosopher said,

—Watch the bumps.

And the Driver closed him snuggly in. The Driver got back into the driver's seat, and I into the back seat. But instead of driving toward the border check, he turned to me and said,

—Looks funny.

He nodded toward the empty passenger seat. I got out of the back seat and into the passenger seat, springy upholstery warmed by a wise backside. As the Driver put the transmission into gear, he said,

—Jason was a thief.

In the warm haze of our headlamps, the austere border crossing appeared. It was marked only by a wooden A-frame sign in the middle of the road and a one-person booth on the shoulder. The sign said, simply, *Stop*. Since every sign is an indication, every indication a reference, every reference a relationship, our relationship was one of waiting patiently before the A-frame sign while a man in the booth finished chewing a sandwich. He waved from the booth, as if nervous to keep us waiting while he wiped his mouth with a napkin.

What the Driver had meant about Jason being a thief had me in something of a knot. I suddenly worried about his intentions. With the soldier now approaching, as we were about to attempt to smuggle a Class Four citizen across a regional border—a restriction the primary function of which was to triage citizens and their wartime affiliations to assess for potential threats to the new peace—this was not the time for me to suddenly worry about the Driver's trustworthiness. Indeed, I should have anticipated such problems before an esteemed man of late middle-age folded himself into the trunk of an automobile.

The soldier was now outside the Driver's window, and the Driver was now rolling down that window. The Driver leaned away from the open window, that crisp air, over to me, his scent like tanning chemicals, bitey in the nostrils, and—I recoiled a bit—he opened the glove compartment. He removed from it his papers. He sat upright again and handed his papers to the soldier. I removed my own papers from the inside pocket of my coat, held them ready for inspection. After the soldier handed the Driver's papers back to him, after he and I conducted the same exchange—returning my papers with a smear of mustard in the margin—he asked,

—Is there anyone else in the car?

The soldier's voice was not incredulous; this was a question he asked countless times each day. But I could see the Driver's knuckles go white on the gear shift. The Driver inhaled. I inhaled. Behind the soldier, through the door of his roadside booth, I could see the butt of a rifle at ease in the corner. The Driver, with the chop of a syllable like an axe into wood, said,

—No.

The soldier moved to the front of the vehicle, and I saw him as if through the wrong end of binoculars as I had not bothered to release my breath; my brain was becoming unready-at-hand. I breathed again. With oxygen bubbling to my brain again, my equilibrium returning, I watched the soldier move the A-frame sign from our path. As the Driver lifted his right foot to the accelerator, the soldier stopped, waved, said,

—One more thing.

He propped the sign against the booth and began walking back to the Driver's window. I impulsively put my hand on the Driver's knee, pushed, hoping to jam his foot down onto the accelerator pedal and zoom us out of this predicament. This action resulted not in our automobile spiriting us to safety but in the Driver swatting my hand away. In the window, the soldier said,

—I almost forgot to warn you. There's a—

And that's when, from the trunk of the automobile, there came a sneeze. A curt, professorial sneeze, but one that still produced two simultaneous effects: The soldier swiveled his head toward the back of the automobile, and my heart found a rhythm fatally unnatural. I attempted to clutch the Driver's hand but he kept pushing it away. Eyes fixed on the rear of the vehicle, the soldier asked,

—What was that?

—Pine marten, the Driver said.

He pointed into the trees around us.

—Forest is filthy with them.

The soldier looked up, squinting into the dark as if it were radiant with light.

—Small, the Driver continued, but decent meat.

Another stifled sneeze came from our cargo in the hold, and the soldier's gaze darted not back to the trunk but rather elsewhere in the trees, the Driver's suggestion having a boomerang effect on the soldier's sense of acoustical orientation.

—You were, the Driver said, about to warn us of something.

The soldier nodded, smiled, and said that there was a report of landmines up ahead so we should take precaution. The Driver thanked him and slowly accelerated across the invisible border. I turned around in my seat to watch that little booth get smaller, and in the moment before the trees closed around it like curtains, the soldier emerged with his rifle.

—Gun, I said.

The Driver shifted into second gear. I heard a crack behind us, the report echoing in the woods. I shouted,

—He's shooting at us!

The Driver kept us in second gear and said,

—Pine martens. Small, but decent meat.

I sat back in my seat. Its cracked leather scraped on the back of my neck. The automobile's headlamps revealed a road swirling between gravel and mud. I said,

—We need to pull over, get him out of the trunk.

In the Driver's silence, in his calm and resolute focus on slowly steering us deeper into the forest, I reminded myself that this man had the chance to alert the soldier to the Philosopher in the trunk, and he'd chosen to protect him, to protect us. I'd been irrational to suspect him, merely for a stray comment.

And, sure enough, when space cleared beside the road, the Driver pulled over. We both got out, inhaling the sweetly dry pine, listening to the now-distant sounds of a soldier hunting a weaselly creature in the dark of night. Above us, stars were emerging, all those constellations describing their vulgar doodles on the blackboard of the sky. The Driver opened the trunk to reveal the Philosopher who, before even stretching out his legs or attempting to hoist himself out, barked from his fetal pretzel and said,

—Landmines? We are driving through landmines?

As he reached for a hand to help him up, he shouted,

—Jesus fucking Christ!

I momentarily took this interjection to be clausal, rather than exclamatory, the first proper noun, *Jesus*, being the active subject that was performing the action of the present participle, *fucking*, with or on the object of the second proper noun, *Christ*. Thankfully, that misapprehension was fleeting, even if the image it painted—which was most upsetting—lingered. But it all seemed oddly apt, as the major premise of the Philosopher's work was that we had made a dire error in thinking of subject as an entity separate from action and object, so his exclamation instructively bound subject, action, and object all together into one wholeness of expression and experience. Jesus fucking Christ, indeed, sir.

With the Philosopher returned to the passenger seat (I was slightly sad to return to the back seat but understood the need, the hierarchy of seat position), and the automobile returned to the forward momentum of the road, things were looking right again. I had, after a brief concern about our guide, confirmed him to be a steadfast fellow; we had made successful passage across the first regional border; the Philosopher and the Driver were engaging in a more free-flowing dialogue than they had initially (they were actually getting on quite well now, having a real intercourse!). The Philosopher was expressing—in language quite distinct from his exacting prose with which I was more familiar, which tucked appositives neatly into dependent clauses like pearls into pockets—concern that we would explode. And the Driver—in syntax less terse than he'd offered me—was assuring him that we would not explode. He was saying,

—I've driven this road uncountable times and have never hit a landmine. That's just something they say. Look at me! Do I look like I've been exploded into bits?

The Philosopher took this question seriously. He looked at the man at the steering wheel, peered through the dark space between them.

—Well, the Philosopher said, I wouldn't know. I didn't know what you looked like before.

And the Philosopher folded his arms over his chest. While the Philosopher had a point—that it remained indeterminate if the form of the Driver as we presently encountered him was a constituent part of a larger, pre-exploded whole, or if he was now, in his apprehendable form, whole—I was inclined to take the perspective of the Driver. While I understood the threat of small terranean explosives tucked into the soil like onion bulbs, I could not imagine actually activating one and so it seemed too remote to be of concern. Indeed, the possibility of us exploding simply did not seem as present as perhaps it should have. During the war, while my peers who were deemed medically fit enough to manage gun and gurney were whisked away, I remained at university (and I cannot say I wasn't relieved!), enjoying the increasingly small class sizes, the increased attention of professors, until a bustling class had been whittled down to an apprentice-mentor situation, with a professor and myself sitting silently in a large lecture hall, each sketching away, the only sound the scrape of charcoal on paper. Around us, empty seats looked on. The people who once filled those seats were not quite abstractions as they were merely absent. The destructed buildings held a pleasing aesthetic to them, seemed arranged more by design than by instruments of doom. Walking that town, I was an archaeologist of the future, unsusceptible to the compulsions and concerns of the present.

The Philosopher was now saying,

—And what of this automobile? How strong is it? Could it withstand a blast? Will it?

The Driver reminded the Philosopher that we were riding in a sedan, not a tank. Regardless, the Philosopher's attention was now fixated on this vehicle. One hand on the dashboard, the other on the linen-lined roof above him, he said,

—This is not of local make. What is this? Not for farming, that's for sure. Tell me, I want to know what kind of casket this is I'll be buried in.

The Driver said, simply,

—It's for transportation.

—Yes, well, of course, but of what?

The Philosopher looked around as if suddenly struck by the alien audacity of this thing that was moving us over the earth, this technology—thinking, surely, of the insidious ways that the technology of modernism fractures experience, the natural environment around us becoming a staging area for the technology, rather than the obverse.

—This car is for transportation, the Driver said, of pleasure.

We rounded a cluster of spruce and the moon flickered through the branches above. The Driver steered with the confidence of someone familiar with the vicissitudes of this road. The Philosopher said,

—And what does that mean? You transport items of pleasure in this vehicle? I take pleasure in the feeling of a fork through a perfectly boiled potato. Tell me, how do you transport that tactile experience in this contraption? Where does it go? In a box in the back seat with the child?

I wondered if I was the child he was referring to, and so this was a vital opportunity to demonstrate my age and maturity: I said,

—I prefer roasted potatoes to boiled.

The conversation in the front seat paused to consider this. Eventually, the Driver said,

—I work for the Madam.

The Philosopher considered this, too, though with a silence of a decidedly different tenor. He looked about his person, realized that his right hand was in direct contact with the upholstery—a porous, absorbent wool—and he retracted his hand, removed the handkerchief from his breast pocket, and wiped his fingers. The movement made brief petals of the paisley silk. The Philosopher asked,

—That is how you know this road?

—Brought women up to the base.

The Driver extended his index finger from the steering wheel to the wooded darkness ahead. Mention of women prompted me to consider my tertiary imperative, that of ensuring I wouldn't be the nubby end of the family line, and the act that it necessitated (or, if family lore was to be believed, did not necessitate, fate willing). But if I was not medically fit enough for military service, how could I be fit enough for carnal service? The shared language between the two endeavors—the conquests, et cetera—suggested shared requirements for participation. I asked,

—Where are the women?

The Driver eyed me in the rearview mirror and the silence that followed made me wonder if the road noise, pebbles pinging the undercarriage, was in fact making audible conversation between front and back seats quite impossible. I was about to repeat myself at a higher volume, when the Philosopher said,

—We should soon be approaching the house of the first chapter of my Part Two.

The Driver, taking a tree-blind turn, said,

—Surely in it reside humans, too, not simply a chapter?

The Philosopher returned his handkerchief to his breast pocket and said,

—It is the house of the first chapter of my Part Two.

He leaned toward the windshield, squinting at the world beyond.

—This infernal road is unrecognizable since I was last here. How do they expect people to navigate without proper signage?

The Driver asked to make sure our destination was, in fact, the house by the coffee mill. The Philosopher confirmed. The Driver said,

—The road to the coffee mill has been redrawn more than the Madam's eyebrows.

The Philosopher let out a yelp of a laugh that succeeded in surprising all three of us, and a second later one wheel hit a divot that wrenched the whole front axle and spun the steering wheel from the Driver's grip. The trees rushed toward us.

It was not until we had all exited the vehicle to assess the trouble we had swerved into that we noticed the centimeter-long cut above the Philosopher's left eye. He removed his handkerchief and blotted his forehead. The Driver was walking around the automobile. We had not, thankfully, hit any trees. The side of the road was a dense moat of mud as wide as I am tall, and it had stopped our tires before the trees could. The mud had already proved too wet for the tread to find purchase and the Driver was now confirming with a flashlight that all four wheels were so mired. The Driver cursed. The Philosopher cursed. I cursed. The Driver because of the mud. The Philosopher because of his gash. And I because of conviviality. The Driver was now rooting through the trunk. Since he'd made room for the Philosopher, the trunk was mostly empty, but he did manage to pull from it, like a magician with a sad rabbit, a small scrap of lumber about the length of my forearm. I approached the Philosopher, careful not to muddy my trousers, and told him that we needed to apply pressure to his wound. I ministered to the Philosopher, until he shouted,

—You're squishing my head like a grape!

I had not meant such harm. His head, after all, was where he kept his thoughts. The Driver told me that when I was done putting the Philosopher in a headlock I should help him get traction. He handed me the length of lumber and told me to wedge it under one of the front tires. I took the wood and crouched beside the fore of the vehicle. As I attempted to follow the Driver's directive, which was dimly actionable at best, I lost sight of the Philosopher. The Driver got back behind the wheel, shouted,

—Contact!

And he hit the accelerator. The wheel in front of me spun and the piece of wood I'd wedged under it shot out like an arrow and hit me square in the forehead. I fell back, briefly entertained the possibility of my death, then felt the cut like a third eye. The automobile had not moved along the horizontal axis at all, but it had slid deeper into the mud. Staunching the small injury on my forehead with my hand, I got to my feet and shouted to the Philosopher,

—Look! I got one too!

But he was walking away. He was trudging into the trees. His steps were unsteady in the mud and roots and rocks. I had never seen an actual tiller make his way over earth unmolested by the modern, but I imagined it looked something like this—not unsteady, actually, just careful, each step considered, placed with clearly articulated intention. I called to him, and he turned and responded to correct me as apparently I'd mistakenly referred to him as a familial, but then he pointed into the trees, and I noticed a few slivers of light between branches. He said,

—That is it! The house!

He kept on toward it. I was about to follow when the Driver grabbed my shoulder and told me to get to work. He told me to find any dry bits of dirt, bark, branches, et cetera, and pile them up behind the front wheels, that this was the only way we'd create traction, then he'd push while I footed the accelerator. The Philosopher had already disappeared through the trees. I began scrounging around for rough, frictive bits of the forest floor, doing as I was told. As I worked, I told the Driver that this sure was exciting. He said,

—Shoving pinecones behind a wheel is exciting to you?

—No, I mean that it's exciting to help shepherd the next great turn in Western philosophy into print. Imagine the ways it will rewrite all that we know.

—Shove some more rocks down beneath the tread, the Driver said.

—Rootlessness, I said, rootlessness and the inauthentic—those are the problems he is resolving in these manuscripts we are rescuing.

—Rescuing, the Driver said. You could say that, I suppose.

We were ready to give it another go, so I sat at the steering wheel and the Driver got behind the automobile. At his cue, I put the transmission into gear, but before I hit the accelerator, I said that being the ones who safeguarded such valuable texts would surely make us widely celebrated. The Driver said,

—Not if they never make it back.

Then he laughed and commanded me to hit the accelerator. I did, and the automobile lurched. I immediately took my foot off the pedal. The Driver began yelling at me, saying it was working and why did I stop? He said we almost had it and needed to throw some more rocks beneath the front wheels. As I began rooting around in the ground like a truffle pig, I was seized by what he'd said—not that I was a damn dunderhead to have stopped accelerating just as we were gaining traction, but that the manuscripts might not make it back. He'd seemed gleeful, almost, at that possibility. Was he planning some sort of sabotage? Perhaps I'd spoken too far ahead of things, as excitement often had me do, when I'd mentioned the texts being valuable and that they had the power to confer celebrity upon us. Was he planning on taking them for himself? Selling them directly to publishers for greater profits than his half of the compensation? Such things were not unheard of: Jan van Eyck's panelpiece *The Just Judges* had still not been returned to its altar in Ghent, having surely netted its thief a hefty profit, and I'd heard tell of other such thefts proliferating in recent months. I said,

—And Jason was not a thief!

I was standing behind the Driver as he crouched at the edge of the road, gathering small stones in his arms. I saw this man now for who he was: a common rascal. Back when he'd pulled my posting from his door, he'd seen an opportunity—not for honest work but for swindle. The Driver looked up; he performed for me a look of confusion and told me to *get to it*. So I did get to it: not the *it* he'd intended, that of my assisting him in the repair of his vehicle to the road, but rather the *it* I now intended, that of my saving the Philosopher and his manuscripts from the ill-intentions of this villain whose pants refused even to cover the totality of his backside. I turned and made haste into the woods, toward those slivers of light.

I keep hoping to see slivers of light emerge in this attic, but I see none. The darkness of night is in conspiracy with these walls. I do not know the time. At our latitude, winter nights can be devastatingly long, summer nights horribly short, but I've never experienced a single evening without the elisions of sleep. The accordion fluctuations of night have always remained abstract until now, as I am compelled to witness every single minute. Regarding what that woman (I'll get to her) said about Bergson's theory of time, that the duration of experience does not align with the measure of the clock, it's easy to not worry too much about that divergence when you have access to the clicks and chimes of a timepiece. Lacking all ways to measure clock time, I now find myself imagining what it could possibly be in contrast to my experience of time passing up here, and the result is that I now have two senses of unstable time—my durational felt time and my imagination of objective time, and the two helix about each other causing me temporal vertigo.

So, without a chronometer, I can attempt to measure my passage to morning by the movement of stars across the frame of that window. The challenge of that, however, is keeping track of which star I am tracking. One cannot label them, after all. My eyes are mostly focused on this page, this typewriter (a Remington Deluxe Model 5), and when I look back up at that little star, as dim as a thought, I wonder if that's the same little star I began tracking. When I doubt myself, the whole process not only confuses my system of time-measurement but, worse, it wastes the time that I'm failing to accurately measure, and then I begin to wonder how this system of measurement even works. What exactly am I measuring between the elusive little star's position in one corner of the window to its (and that *it* is alleged, since I cannot ascertain the *it*ness of that star, and all deictics' relationships to their referents are obviously shaky at best) current position a quarter of the way across the window? What, in other words, does that passage correspond to? What, for that matter, does a Greenwich-verified minute correspond to? This whole damn thing of time is beginning to seem like a shell game, a complex series of measurements, all nestled into each other, that don't ultimately correspond to anything other than themselves. I renounce the whole grift. I don't need the click of a second hand to count time when I have the clack of these keys. Here, then, is how long it took me to walk from the ditch-driven automobile to the house where I was to track down the Philosopher: not this collection of minutes but this pile of words.

On the other side of a mild density of trees, I approached the country house that apparently held the first chapter of the Philosopher's Part Two. The house was half-timbered (a common though shockingly vulgar aesthetic in these rural parts, as those exposed beams always appeared to me like garters seen under one's skirts), illuminated from within, each window a little ornament of golden light. The texture of that light suggested not electrical illumination but that by tallow and wick. I hesitated before the front door, noting with shame that I had not succeeded in keeping my trousers free of mud. My eyes adjusted to the contrast between the light in the doorside window and the darkness in which I stood, and in that window I saw the Philosopher framed as if in a portrait. His posture was a bit more erect than I'd seen it before, lending to this sense of the presentational. It was a shame that he moved, spoiling the illusion of his being so nicely captured in the materials of my art, but he moved to glance into the camera obscura, so to speak, and wave at me. In a moment, the front door opened.

In the doorway stood a man of perhaps my age, in a sweater too long and a hairstyle too short. He had a checkmark scar on his forehead, and his scowl was not that of the average ruralite; this was a glare earned not from years squinting against the sun but from years of skeptical eyemaking at strangers. He took a moment to acknowledge the forehead wounds of the Philosopher and myself (neither too deep, thank goodness). This young man's expression was one that demanded of me my credentials and intentions for arriving at his door. The Philosopher, however, intervened, stepping between us with an explanation that I was his assistant (I would have preferred associate) and valet. The young man accepted my entrance, granting that I make thorough use of the boot-scraper beside the door, and I obliged, sloughing smooth peels of mud from my soles.

Inside, the walls were decorated with the preserved busts of the local fauna, not just the antlered beasts, but those in and around the weasel family, too, and I was oddly impressed that this home's display featured a far more representative sampling than one would typically expect. Across from the wood-burning stove, black and pot-bellied, a table was freshly set with a stout bottle of clear liquid, two small glasses beside. The young man walked over to the shelf and found a third for the tableau. He poured what smelled to be turpentine into all three. He picked up one glass, the Philosopher the second. I belatedly picked up the third. I followed their lead in swallowing my serving, but they did not follow my lead in suppressing a burning retch, lips clenched against fist, eyes like cigarette cherries. I felt the Philosopher's hand on my back, patting. The Philosopher said,

—You were saying that your father has passed? I don't understand why I didn't hear of this. He was a confidant of mine, your father. A great man.

The young man said,

—He was heretical.

Blood drained from my head, not from the intrafamilial tension on display but from the violent-tasting beverage I'd just imbibed. I groped around for something and found the back of a chair. I managed to sit myself down at the table, prop my head up in my hands. The Philosopher, perhaps relieved to focus on me for a moment, said,

—My assistant might need a receptacle.

The young man continued:

—And he kept heretical associations.

The Philosopher placed a vase before me. I understood this was for me to make sick into. To the young man, he said,

—Our relationship was largely built around mutual enthusiasm for lawn billiards.

The young man removed my vomit vase and said,

—That's a bit of an heirloom.

He replaced it with a cast iron pot, for which I thanked him, but I was beginning to regain my sense of things. The young man said,

—That is why I am heretical.

He smiled, pleasurelessly, as if simply showing his teeth to a dentist.

—And I keep heretical associations myself. He wrote to me and requested I return. I made the trip. By the time I arrived, he was dead.

Wishing to join the discussion, I said,

—Windy die?

The young man looked at me with some confusion and asked me to repeat myself.

—When did he die?

The young man said April. I asked how, as the basic facts of such things seemed a perfectly reasonable matter for conversation, though the Philosopher's look suggested otherwise. The young man said,

—Cyanide. Still smelled like soured almonds when I returned.

The Philosopher sat beside me at the table and nodded, offering further condolences. The young man said that he was keeping all of his father's important effects in the upstairs study, as it was nice for him to sit with them, sift through the material and see the world as his father saw it.

—But I got this.

The young man motioned to an envelope held on the counter beneath a large stein.

—They're confiscating his possessions.

He handed the letter to the Philosopher who eyed it as if it were an alien communique. I wondered if this young man might be our solution to the problem of our Driver. If he had a vehicle we might borrow for the evening, we could leave the Driver and his scheming, thieving ways.

—And when they come for his effects, the young man said, I'll be ready.

I asked him,

—With an automobile, perhaps?

He pulled from his belt not a jangly set of keys but the shiny serration of a hunting knife. He said,

—First man to lay finger on my father's things, I'm going to gut from scrotum to gullet. Unzip like a duffel bag.

The Philosopher, with a fluttering of whatsits previously unheard in his speech, reintroduced the topic of lawn billiards, both in and of itself and as a metonym of all lawn sports. Eventually, the young man said,

—Pause there a moment. I have a photograph of my father with his mallet. I will find it for you.

He excused himself into a room just off the kitchen, and as soon as he was out of sight, the Philosopher grabbed me by the arm, put his face close enough for me to be tickled by his breath, and he said,

—Find a reason to go upstairs. In the study, retrieve for me my chapter.

Half my brain was still thinking of how to tell him about the deception of the Driver and our need for a new mode of transport, but instead I asked how I could possibly know what was what in a room I'd never been in before, looking for a manuscript I had never seen. The Philosopher said,

—The man was functionally illiterate. If you see words on a page, it was not by or for him. Grab it. And be quiet about it. These old farmhouses moan like hogs in estrus.

The young man came back into the room and the Philosopher let go of my arm. The young man did, in fact, have a photograph of his father posing with a croquet mallet, and the Philosopher made a great deal of fuss about it. I was quite relieved to have the focus be something other than death and its implements, so I participated in the discussion of the photograph—the best time of year for croquet, one's preferences for play partners—until the Philosopher gave me a swift kick to the shin beneath the table and I yelped. To cover for my outburst, I said I needed to use the commode. The young man directed me toward the water room just off the kitchen. I said,

—I would prefer to use a toilet on the second floor.

When prompted to explain, I said,

—I am unable to make water within audible radius of others, so, if possible, I would like to repair upstairs for my relief.

The young man said that the house did, in fact, have a toilet upstairs, but that I would have to hold the flusher until all went down. I told him that I would be honored to do so.

With the help of a small candelabra, I found a very short hallway that concluded at a window, and on each side was a door. With only two rooms, then, it seemed simple enough to find the dead man's study. My readings in the Philosopher's discipline seemed to have prepared me (not just prepared me, but galvanized me) for the binary, either/or choice of two doors: Does one choose the aesthetic life or the ethical life, the inauthentic life or the authentic, the left door or the right? Indeed, my readings seemed to have presented all of life as a choice between two doors. But, on the other hand (ah, another tempting binary, stowing away in received language!), these were just doors, and if I selected the wrong one, I could merely turn around and select the other one. I picked the door to my right—not, I realized, out of robust and rational deliberation, but simply because my dominant hand is the hand that is my right, and so it felt natural to reach for the door that was to my right. Behind it was a toilet. So I closed it and reached for the opposite door.

Inside, I saw a small room cluttered with objects: objects, I saw as I stepped in, as these objects moved from the general to the specific, that were largely nautical in origin, decorative in application, a sextant on a shelf, wooden pulleys like knuckly fists, the scent of wood polish about. I sat at the roll-top desk perched beside the window and unrolled the roll-top. I placed the three-candle candelabra on top of the desk and opened the top drawer: It was filled not with a treatise on the complications of existence but with a robust assortment of pornographic postcards from, by my estimate, the age of Victoria and the Tsars. I made this estimate based on the texture of the filmstock and the elaborate nature of the hats. Although now that I was thinking about it, it's not entirely true to say these images were not grappling with existence: The spirit of invention and the vigor of determination were evident on their performers' sallow faces; here was the dialectic in peak tension, the thesis, the antithesis, the pushing toward some synthesis that always seemed to occur just after the flash of the camera. The collection of classic smut continued in the next drawer, and the next. The shelves were occupied by wooden milk crates that contained still more, though these had clearly been subject to less care, their glossy prints showing greater wear.

Further into the archive, beneath a crate of images that prominently featured parasol-centric activities, I found, at last, something the size of a manuscript, folded in butcher paper and wrapped in twine. I placed it on my lap, judged the contents to be roughly between eighty and a hundred pages, the warm weight of a small cat, a comparison I could almost believe if it were not for the crinkling of the paper. I opened the package as if it were a Christmas present, and, sure enough, there in my hands, was the first chapter of the Philosopher's Part Two. The pages were a mix of typewritten and handwritten, some pages featuring an argumentative cluster of both, as if a vigorous debate were being staged between not just modes of Being but modes of composition, the techno-modern of the typewriter versus the superannuated of the cursive. The black typewritten letters had a ghostly trace of deep sky blue. I read what I could in the time that I had and was immediately stimulated by the intensity of what I saw.

Although a text like that was not meant to be understood on first read—much less first skim while under duress—it was less the contents and more the formal aspects of the language that were immediately striking: the coyness of a small observation, an observation begging for closer attention, attention that grew tumescently into a question, a question with the force of an assertion, an assertion that found assumptions I never knew I had and penetrated them with devastating force. The pressure of the manuscript on my lap was becoming both urgent and unbearable, and that's when I noticed the interruption outside the window.

The Driver was standing below, flashlight in hand, waving up at me, having surely seen my candle-lit figure in the window. He did not suspect what I suspected of him, so his wave appeared naïve, stupid. What choice did I have but to accept his help? The Philosopher had sent me up here to retrieve his chapter without consideration of how I would safeguard it out of the house. Although I felt I should not trust the Driver, I knew I could not trust the young man downstairs—the young man who seemed well trained in the art of dressing game animals both large and small and had an interest in taxidermying them into decorative ghouls. I needed to preserve this manuscript, this vital artifact of Western Civilization, this rope cast down into Plato's cave to help yank us blind fools up into the light; I also needed to preserve my own bodily integrity. The oblique and cryptic threat of the man outside was still more inviting than the explicit and eager threat of the man downstairs. Either/or, door one or door two—even with the answer obvious, I couldn't make it. I was too worked up to think, and I calmed myself momentarily with the dead man's effects.

Then, finding a firm resolve, I bound the manuscript back together, making a tight but looping knot with the twine. I opened the window, its creak giving me a shiver of dread. I silently returned the wave of the Driver, held the wrapped pages up for him to see. Lit only by the dim light of the house (he'd turned his flashlight off to avoid detection, I suspect), his expression was not visible, but he seemed to understand, as without a sound he moved directly beneath the window and gestured for me to drop the package down to him. I held it out, briefly wondered if I was about to drop this into the arms of a thief, if I would turn out to be the last person to read its words, then I let go.

Downstairs, my host and my passenger looked at me with some worry. The young man in particular wanted to know if everything was all right. I said yes, I was quite well, thank you, but the young man continued in his expressions of concern. He said that healthy micturition in a male still within the age of conscription should not take as long as I took. I said I took no longer than was normal. The young man said,

—Those candles were as tall as your face when you walked up those stairs, and now they're as small as your thumbs.

It was true, the candles in my candelabra had reduced in size considerably, and the wax had made a mess of the engraving of the god Loge on the handle, or maybe that was just the vicissitudes of the material that I mistook for a face. Either way, the young man was now saying,

—I knew a medic who cleared up a painful piss with a tincture of arsenic.

As the young man stepped toward me, the Philosopher seemed to retreat into the walls; in my visual periphery, his image blurred with that of the stuffed badger. The young man relieved me of the candelabra, placing it on the table, and he motioned for me to sit.

—I have some in my cabinet, the young man said.

He went over to the kitchen cabinet and began rooting around in the teas and spices.

—I keep it labeled *chamomile* for safekeeping.

He picked up small tins, shook them, sniffed them. While his back was turned, I tried to silently communicate to the Philosopher (who was standing timidly beneath not a badger but a wolverine) the situation as it had evolved: that the Driver was now outside, and that he had the manuscript (having initially fumbled it into a row of onion sprouts before quickly recovering it and dusting the soil from its butcher-paper wrapping). Instead of nodding, signaling that he understood all that I had accomplished and communicated, the Philosopher just glared at me and swatted.

—And here we go. Lovely.

The young man was bringing a single teacup, rattling lightly on a mismatched saucer, over to the table. The steaming liquid it held was a yellowish beige and redolent of dead flowers. I asked if that was chamomile, and the young man just said,

—Helps it metabolize.

I looked with trepidation at the Philosopher who nodded at me and gestured sipping. I assured the young man that I had no need for chemical intervention in my bladder or surrounding systems, but he said the one thing you don't want to turn your back on is infection. Then he added a footnote:

—Well, that and a capuchin with a gun.

The Philosopher said,

—The monks are arming themselves?

And the young man said,

—Not monk. Mon*key*. A gunner I knew kept a capuchin as a pet. Gave the creature his nine-millimeter to play with. We all posed for pictures with it—like Bonnie and Clyde. It was perfectly good fun, until the monkey shot an engineer.

The Philosopher, stepping toward the table with an offer of consoling wisdom, said that accidents happen.

—Then he shot a colonel, the young man continued, and a cook, then the gunner himself. That cute little shit took down half our regiment before he was neutralized.

The young man lowered his head in apparent observance of those lost to interspecies violence. Then he raised his head, looked at me, and said,

—Drink up.

And I did. So distracted by the tale of an insurgent monkey was I that when I heard the imperative to *drink up* and I looked down and saw the warm cup of tea, I acted on a sense of propriety and muscle memory and took a sip. It wasn't until I swallowed that sip that I realized what I'd done. (I tasted only the chamomile tea; I thought death would taste a bit more acrid.)

I jerked away from the table. I shouted that we must be going. And I ushered the old man, the great man, to the door. As I did so, he offered the young man apologies for the unsociable behavior of his assistant and he again offered condolences for the loss of the young man's father, though by that time we were back outside and searching in the darkness for the Driver.

Holding the Philosopher by the crook of his arm, I pulled him in the direction of the automobile. We quickly encountered not the relief of the road through the trees but the gnarl of branches against our faces. The Philosopher grunted with displeasure and twisted his arm from my grasp. He demanded to know where the Driver was, where the automobile was, where his manuscript was. I told him the automobile was around here somewhere, that we must be close, and that the Driver had the manuscript. But even as I said that, I worried that I was wrong, that the Driver had absconded with both the manuscript and the automobile, leaving us alone in the woods with a potential mad man—me with poison coursing through my veins and the world without the Philosopher's tract. I did not express those concerns. Instead, I expressed my assurances that all was going perfectly according to plan. The Philosopher barked,

—Then show me my manuscript.

It was right this way, I told him and took him by the hand and led him into the darkness. I attempted to walk confidently, each step intended to inspire confidence, and I was doing a fairly good job of this—which is to say I was starting to feel genuinely confident, and the Philosopher was following along—until my foot met a root and I fell open-mouthed into the mud. The

Philosopher did not offer any assistance and I got to my knees spitting pine needles from my tongue. I heard,

—Not going to find it down there.

I assumed this was the voice of the Philosopher until I heard the Philosopher respond with a gasp of relief. I cleared the mud from my eyes and saw, holding a flashlight in one hand and the manuscript in the other, the Driver standing above me.

By the time we'd followed the Driver back to the automobile, which he'd managed to get back onto the road, the Driver and the Philosopher were in a bit of a bicker. The Driver got back behind the wheel and the Philosopher sat beside him saying,

—Give it here. Give it to me.

He made grabbing motions with his hands, but the Driver kept the manuscript clutched tight to his side, blocking the Philosopher's reach with his shoulder. The Philosopher was saying,

—You give that to me, you whoremonger. That is my work! I have come too far to have my work manhandled by someone who pedals syphilis across the country.

And the Driver was saying,

—All I'm saying is that this little storybook of yours has already caused me considerably more hassle than I signed up for and a *thank you* for my efforts, which have been beyond my job description, would be nice!

And I was saying,

—I seem to have consumed a lethal substance and I would very much appreciate some medical attention.

And the Philosopher was saying,

—Countless hours! Countless hours I have given to those pages, and I will not have them saved from the eyes and hands of enemy forces only to see them clutched away and carelessly bent like they were some pulp entertainment.

And the Driver was saying,

—And my vehicle has sustained scrapes beyond what I anticipated. If you saw the magazine advertisement for this car, you would see the words *cosmopolitan cruiser*, and in it I drive people of respect—and you.

And I was saying,

—The poison might very well be coursing through my blood, on its way to my heart at this moment, or my brain. To be honest, I'm not sure what organ arsenic attacks, but whatever its aims it is surely getting closer to achieving them.

And the Philosopher was saying,

—You surely have no idea what the work is that you are now molesting in your grip. That's not some Mickey Mouse runabout or penny-dreadful bodice-ripper, I can tell you that. It is a very serious work and I am a very serious man and you should heed me!

And the Driver was saying,

—And people of respect give respect, and that means simply offering gratitude when it is called for. Can't you do something as simple as admit that a man of my work has helped you?

And I was saying,

—I am feeling an increased heart-rate and my brow is sweaty. Are these not the symptoms of arsenic poisoning?

And the Driver, looking back at me—someone finally looking at me—said,

—Arsenic poisoning?

And the Philosopher said,

—Bah! It was nothing but a sip! Diluted in tea. A tincture for his syphilis.

And I said,

—I do not have syphilis!

And the Driver said,

—A tincture should clear it up just fine. You will be fine.

And the Philosopher said,

—That's what I said. Thank you.

And the Driver said,

—You're welcome! See? A bit of gratitude is all I wanted.

And the Driver handed the manuscript to the Philosopher who said,

—Well, I was waiting for you to give the manuscript back before I gave a thank-you.

And the Driver said,

—And I'm not some man-child who does not know what that is you're holding. I know you. I know your work. I know that's not an issue of *Spicy Investigator* you're writing.

The Driver brushed dirt from his coat and continued:

—But it wouldn't kill you to add some steamy bits.

And I said,

—I find it quite stimulating.

And the Philosopher, peeking into the butcher paper to confirm its contents, said, quietly, as if to himself,

—Maybe I will. And *Spicy Investigator* was not dreck.

And the Driver said,

—You read *Spicy Investigator*?

And the Philosopher said,

—When I was in primary, it was all you could get to read around here. It was called *Super Investigator* then, and it did not have any pictures. They switched it to *Spicy* when their distribution changed.

And the Philosopher smirked, his mustache twitching, then continued:

—But it was always spicy.

And then a spasm of shame seemed to tighten him back up. He said,

—It was always a good publication. In those stories is where I first discovered induction, deduction. The syllogistic, predicate logic—it's all in those tales of figuring out who brained whom and why.

And the Driver said,

—Was T.R. Wolf writing for it back when it was *Super*?

And the Philosopher said,

—Yes, but T.R. Wolf does not exist.

And the Driver said,

—What do you mean?

And the Philosopher said,

—A *nom de plume*. Thousands have been T.R. Wolf over the years. You can always tell. For example, when Lydia the Liontamer's story concluded not with her return to Algiers but with her *rapprochement* with the Fat Man.

And the Driver said,

—That made no sense!

And the Philosopher said,

—That was a new writer! A new T.R. Wolf, one who didn't even bother to read the first installments of the story he was taking over.

The Driver slouched in heartbreak and said,

—I never knew.

From the back seat, I said,

—Do either of you enjoy John Ruskin's volumes of *Modern Painters*? It's also a serialization, of sorts.

The Driver rubbed his arms; he turned the engine over, turned on the headlamps, then held his hands over the heating vents in the console. He said,

—I always imagined getting to meet T.R. Wolf.

The Philosopher said,

—You've probably met one of them at some point or another.

The Driver chuckled. Then no one said anything. The crickets etched little notes into the silence. In the distance, we heard a scream. The Driver wondered aloud if it was a wildcat. Then the scream came again, with a distinct human timbre, the stops of syllables. The Philosopher said,

—Whoever that is, he's getting closer.

And that's when we saw him: Straight ahead of us, on the road, emerging into the light of our headlamps, the young man was running toward us, brandishing a pistol, and screaming,

—Thieves! Stop, thieves!

The Philosopher clutched his manuscript. The young man, rapidly approaching, fired a single shot at us, hitting the hood. The Driver rushed to get the automobile in gear.

—Stop, you thieves!

The engine stalled out. The young man aimed his pistol again, and even though it wobbled as he ran at us, I could still see the hollow of the barrel as clear as anything I've ever seen. And that's when his body exploded.

I must pause here to welcome a new associate into my writing attic. Or actually, not a new associate at all. An old associate. It seems that the Chemist's cat (whose formal introduction will have to wait for the proper moment in this kinked chronology) has somehow managed to follow us here. Again, I cannot begin to imagine how he did it—whether by hiding out in the automobile (how?) or by running along after us (how?)—but he is here. A few moments ago, he sidled up to the window and began pawing on the glass. The sound of retracted claws and little paw pads on glass is an oddly specific one. I went to the window and attempted to open it, but it was stuck shut. As I struggled to pull the window up, the cat licked at the glass down near my hands. I soon saw that someone had applied a gummy coat of paint, covering the seam between window and frame. I gestured to the cat, who regarded me with skepticism, and I went back to this table, returning with a pen, which I applied to the paint-sealed juncture. When I was finally able to open the window, the cat, offering no nuzzle of gratitude or even a sign of recognition from our previous adventures this evening, slunk into the room. He—and I have assumed it to be a he, though I have not deigned to check—quickly perched beside this typewriter, teased the carriage lever with his tail. I closed the window and returned to this table.

His fur is cold. He has offered my wrist his teeth, but ineffectually, affectionatelyy. He has paraded over this keyboard many times now, though only one step was heavy enough to depress a letter, a superfluous *y* that I retain there to mark his contributions. And what of his contributions? What of my contributions? Perhaps the odd typographical error is all we'll have to show, a smudge. If we're lucky. But, like me, his presence is not merely on the page now but of the page, as that is where I might exert a modicum of control. Walking away, he shows me the dark asterisk of his under-tail. Offered this display, I will try to keep my eyes on this page. He is now in the corner swatting at a moth of his own imagination. That is well and good. I do not want him to see what I have to type next.

The whole front part of our automobile was covered in the young man's blood. There were thicker bits of material, too, though from the inside of the sedan, those bits were harder to identify with much certainty. The ringing in my ears was not so much a ringing as it was a distancing, the audible world taking a few steps back. In the front seat, the Philosopher was holding one shaking hand up at the windshield—which was intact, save for a few diacritic cracks—as if trying to touch the viscous red that was safely on the other side of the glass, while with his other hand he gripped his manuscript to his chest like it was a baby. The Driver turned on the windshield wipers and the young man's insides smeared but did not clear; indeed, the blood had an adhesive quality like glue. While the mess was all on the outside, and we were safely sealed inside glass and metal, we could still smell it: the sulfuric char and the cloying gore, wafting in through the open heater vents. The Driver attempted to close the vents, but the heady odor was already inside.

The Driver opened his door and retched into the dirt. He started to get out of the vehicle, but—and with the smear on the windows, this part was opaque to me—he must have seen something that urged him back in. He closed the door and gripped the steering wheel and shouted for the Philosopher to not open his door, as apparently he'd made overtures to exiting as well. The Driver quickly turned over the engine again and successfully engaged the transmission. He drove ahead, blindly, still unable to see through the mess on the windshield, cranking the wheel dramatically to the right, describing a semicircle in the road. As we drove onward, the Driver attempting to squint through the impenetrable smear of horror on the glass, the Philosopher noticed that the seal around the Driver's door was itself bleeding. In his brief foray out of the automobile, the Driver had allowed the blood to seep in, and a thick chord of the stuff lined the inside of his door, gathering in red pearls that quivered with the bumps in the road, and when one such pearl became a drop that, unseen by the Driver but watched intently by the Philosopher, fell onto the Driver's forearm, the Philosopher said words that I could not hear but that moved his mouth like a prayer. The Driver, perhaps realizing that we were surely to collide with a tree if he continued in this way, pulled to a stop. He turned around in his seat and took hold of me, one hand on my shirt collar. The way his other hand wrapped around my mouth suggested that I had been screaming. The Philosopher clutched his own mouth and tried to put his head down, but the Driver saw this, let go of me, and with one hand reached over the Philosopher to open his door, and with the other hand pushed the man to point his head out, and the Philosopher made sick onto the side of the road. Presumably, the Driver had been able to drive far enough from the blast of the landmine to get away from whatever he'd seen, because he now encouraged us, rather forcefully, to get out.

Now in the road, I could see that the automobile appeared as if its front end had been dipped in cherry-chocolate sauce, only a cherry-chocolate sauce that smelled rather of burning sewage. For reasons I didn't understand, from the inside, the splatter had appeared a far more vibrant red, while on the outside that red was maroon and streaked with brown and black. Most of the chunkier bits of material had fallen off, though there were some clots resting in the nook between hood and windshield. Behind us, the road was dark, and whenever I looked back in that direction the Driver scolded me to look away. The automobile's headlamps were the only light, filtered red. The Driver approached me and delivered to my face a few slaps that again suggested I'd been screaming. The Philosopher was cowering away to the side of the road, seeking cover behind a tree. The Driver demanded that I remove my coat. I did so, and he removed his. In a moment of inspiration that I would not fully appreciate until later, I removed from the inside pocket my papers. The Driver took our coats and began wiping down the hood, the windshield, the roof, the bumper—wherever the automobile's outside featured the young man's insides. His efforts, though enthusiastic, hardly seemed effective. The blood was so viscous that it could not simply be wiped away; worse, in the Driver's attempt to do so, the gore was gathering pine needles and other bits of earth—so many pine needles, in fact, that the front end of the automobile soon had the prickly quality of a porcupine. Rushing toward the Driver, the Philosopher shouted,

—Stop it! You are making it worse! Can you not see that you are making it worse?

The Driver continued with determination. The Philosopher attempted to stop him, grabbing his arm. The manuscript fell to the ground. While the older man attempted to stop the younger man from using wool coats, which now had the appearance of roadkill, to clean the gore from our automobile, I walked over to the manuscript, still wrapped in butcher paper, though with one fold undone, exposing the first typewritten page, and I picked it up, brushed the dirt off. The Driver said,

—We cannot cross any checkpoints looking like this!

The Philosopher said,

—We need water to clean it. Where can we get water?

I unwrapped the manuscript a bit more and, crouched on the ground, read snatches of its blue-penumbra'd language: *The ethos of the modern is fragmentation, a natural state of the rootless, and as art seeks to reveal truth beyond itself, it is naturally predicated on cohesion.* The Driver was saying that we were more than twenty kilometers from the nearest natural water source, but that the Madam's house was no more than ten, maybe twelve kilometers from here. The Philosopher scoffed; he would not let this quest get derailed into such ribaldry. Besides, the next house, the Chemist's house, was just a couple kilometers into the next region. *To seek comprehension of the fragmentary is to seek cohesion of what does not cohere; thus the act of art to seek comprehension is an act of aggression to its forces.*

—We have to go on foot, I said. The two of us with our travel papers. We will cross on foot.

I stood up, clutching the manuscript. To the Philosopher, I said,

—Without a trunk to hide in, you will have to stay here with the automobile.

The Philosopher saw that I had unwrapped the butcher paper and he took the manuscript from me. He then looked me in the eye and said,

—You expect me to trust you to walk into the home of my associate and ask for my manuscript?

I asked him if he hadn't already trusted me. He said that my task in the young man's house was under his supervision and direction, that I had not yet earned his complete trust. I told him,

—You will trust me, then, after I do this thing for you. Trust is a product of exchange, not a precondition for it.

He barked at me, spittle misting my face, and said,

—That's hogwash. I will trust you because I have no choice. And compelled trust is not trust. Now go get my manuscript, and, dear God, you're pissing yourself.

After clearing the windshield enough for the Driver to see the road, after we drove almost all the way to the next regional border, after stopping just shy of that border and leaving the Philosopher in the automobile, and the automobile tucked behind some trees just off the road, the Driver and I set off on foot— toward the checkpoint and the Chemist's house beyond, in which I was to retrieve chapter two of the Philosopher's Part Two. The Philosopher had given me very precise instructions, which I was now, walking down a single-lane dirt road alongside the Driver, incanting silently to myself (or not so silently, if the sidelong glares from the Driver were to be believed). When we had left the Philosopher, he had stationed himself in the front seat with his manuscript on his lap, removed a pen from his pocket, unscrewing its cap, and said he would use the time to make some marginalia on his recovered chapter under the interior dome light of the automobile, and now I was walking down this road, which was physically uncomfortable to traverse, as my crotch was still drying in the cold mountain air (and I had tried unsuccessfully to convince the Philosopher that the ease with which I had wetted myself roadside was proof that I had no such infectious condition that had necessitated that tincture of arsenic), but also psychically uncomfortable, as this road had proven quite explosive, and I wished I'd had the Philosopher here with me for some counsel, specifically on the possibility that I imagined with every step, that of death.

I considered something I'd read of his in the months when my classrooms were clearing out with alarming speed and I first realized that I (after my aunt) would be the last of a familial line: The Philosopher contended that, despite the rituals of grief, death is always inward-turning, which is to say the death of others is only significant to us in how it relates to my own death, as the death of others is always observational, never participatory, which meant that every step I took that did not trigger a landmine was a reminder not necessarily of my own Being but essentially of my own isolation in that Being. (We were now approaching the checkpoint for the border of the next region, the soldier stepping out of his little booth with his hand raised, and with his eyebrows raised, about to ask us why we were walking along such a road at night, the Driver about to respond.) And what of the fact of death's compulsory solipsism? The Philosopher argued that, following from his first premise, death is precisely what gives meaning to experience, as infinite experience would negate the need for meaning in the teleological sense, even while it (death) is the thing we never experience, in that, since we do not live through death, we cannot report on it, implying experience is predicated on the reflection of anamnesis—not the moment of neomnesis and certainly not the anticipation of promnesis—meaning that *meaning* is only made after the moment of action, and maybe all this was going to be further expounded upon in Part Two, which, either way, meant that every step I took that did not trigger a landmine was also an affirmation of meaning but only insofar as I would be around to reflect on that experience. (And after I handed my papers to the soldier, he took note of a small smear of red near the state seal and examined this smear in a patch of copper light, at which point the Driver claimed it was just the result of a shaving incident, and wasn't it so hard to find a well-made straight edge these days, and here, the soldier should now look over the Driver's papers.) And what of the fact that, as one cannot report on death, its precise nature is unknown? The Philosopher argued that, following from his second premise, death is both certain and uncertain, uncertain both in the sense of its aforementioned unreportability and in the unpredictable temporicity of its event, in that we never really know when it will occur, which meant that every step I took that did not trigger a landmine was fraught with the, as he says, possibility of the impossible. (And as we walked away from the soldier's little roadside booth, the soldier himself remaining in the road to observe us walking on into the night, the Driver increased his speed, attempting to maintain the appearance of calm walking while accelerating to the pace of running, urging me with little bumps to the arm and shoulder to keep up with him.) And what of the fact of death's certain uncertainty? The Philosopher concluded that, following from his first, second, and third premises, true authenticity is not freeing oneself from the burden of death, but rather embracing it, that existence is a matrix of contingency. To be aware, then, that at any moment I could explode into bits was for me to be my true self.

I tried explaining this to the Driver, and he told me I was a fool. The Driver pushed me onto the grassy bank sloping up from the road. He said landmines would be less likely in the undergrowth. Although the Driver definitely had a good point here, trudging through grass and bushy things, all of which was unseen by me since the Driver was keeping his flashlight trained on his own path, I found the dark unknowable nature of my steps—the scrape of branch like a rodent's claw, the tickle of leaf like a snake's caress, and always the possibility of a squishy slug underfoot—somehow more viscerally upsetting than the potential buried in the road. I asked the Driver why he was not more curious about the wisdom our passenger had to offer, and he responded that if the Philosopher wanted to properly investigate death, he should ask the countless people whose death he helped expedite. The Driver asked,

—Why do you think he's not able to cross regional borders himself?

—Because he's been listed as Class Four, I said.

—And why is he listed as Class Four?

—That's just bureaucracy, something for the pencil-pushers to sort out, a form that needs to be filed.

—He was affiliated. That's not a mere error.

—The affiliation was a mere requirement of his rectorship. It was part of his job.

—Would you keep that job?

—That's a silly question! A position like that was more than just a job. It was stability, the only way to work with students, to shape the intellectual future of the country, and beyond.

—He certainly did that.

The Driver pushed a branch out of his way. The flashlight in his hand animated the trees ahead of us. He said,

—His influence was a bit beyond what I suspect he thought the classroom could provide.

—But the classroom is inherently apolitical!

—Did it occur to you that he could have taken a position anywhere, and yet he stayed?

—That position wasn't just anywhere, I explained. It was here. These lands are where he was born, where he was raised. He wrote about these mountains, these trees, the ways they've fostered centuries of a moral, aesthetic, and intellectual character.

—Whose moral, aesthetic, and intellectual character?

I saw what he was getting at, but I insisted that was misapprehending the nature of the They that the Philosopher warned of. The Driver said,

—So those he fired from their academic positions, they were—

—Those were just the requirements of his job, I said.

—Yes, yes, so those he fired, those he delivered into the hands of the brutes, not *their* moral, aesthetic, and intellectual character, I presume.

—Well, no. First of all, I suspect those rumors are not accurate. But, to your point, according to the Philosopher, the conditions—historical, even mythic in their scope—those are contingent. We are products, naturally, of this landscape, this history. I mean, I suppose I poke a bit of fun at these rural parts, but these trees are quite lovely, and I do feel an affinity for them.

—Yes, yes, the Driver said. I know that pitch: the windmill, the spindle and loom, the hills like tits, the tits like hills.

—Yes, the country as the body of the people.

—Ah, throw in a few dragons while you're at it.

—Well, actually, there is some new archeological credence to many of those legends, some of which do feature dragons.

—It's boyish fantasy, you twit.

But, I contended—stumbling over a root and quickly recovering myself—this was all just hearsay about the requirements of his post. The real work he had been producing for decades, that was the real him. And that work was exquisite in its—

—Bullshit, the Driver said. Bootlicking bullshit. I know all about this man, his work. When you pounded that piece of paper to my door and sputtered his name, it was not the first time I'd encountered it, believe me. And I don't just mean because he's the one man in a fifty kilometer radius of the Madam's house who has yet to pay a visit, no.

I asked if the Driver was familiar not just with the Philosopher's reputation but with his oeuvre.

—His oeuvre? I'm familiar with his—what should I call it?—justifications. His project of justifying the unjustifiable.

That sounded like a quote of the Philosopher's, justifying the unjustifiable; it had the chiasmic turn that he was so fond of in his writing, but the Driver ignored this point of mine and said,

—He spent all those years and all those pages building elaborate edifices of meaning and Being, all on the foundation of selfishness.

—Not selfishness! Self-authentication.

—All that means is that a person is only responsible to himself, not to others.

—That's not how I would put it, and besides, his writing is academic, not popular—to most, after all, his work is unreadable!

—When you create justifications for acting with impunity, people will pay attention, and always the wrong people.

—Well, his *real* readership is far more nuanced in their thinking.

—He made them think all that is important is achieving whatever the self deems important. All that talk of freedom, but to who, to what? To what one wants, not what the world needs. And that means no right, no wrong. All freedom and no obligation—it's juvenile, just a paean to power. Freedom to seize power, with no obligation to challenge it. And you know what that lack of obligation really is?

—Authenticity!

—It's silence. *That's* the highest form of speech, according to that man. To remain silent. Can you imagine? A virtue.

—His thinking on the matter of silence is more complex than that, surely.

—He built a system of permission, and those who needed it used it. He built a system of passivity, and those who needed it used it. When classrooms refuse to characterize events in terms of what is right and what is wrong—

—Apolitical!

—That's when the brutes take over. And when those who granted permission think silence is the pinnacle of thought and expression, that's when the brutes get impunity.

I struggled to keep up with the Driver and his flashlight. After focusing on my walking through the underbrush, I closed the gap between us and said that all that may be true, but it does not mean that he was complicit in any crimes, in any actual atrocities, of which I certainly knew nothing. The Driver stopped, turned, shone the flashlight into my eyes.

—Don't be stupid.

—I am not stupid! I am a student at a well-respected university! Where, might I ask, did you do your schooling? Where, might I ask, did you come up with all these baseless accusations about a great intellectual whose work is a bit more challenging to grasp than *Saucy Investigator*?

He took the flashlight away from my eyes.

—That's *Spicy Investigator*, and you'd be surprised. That car back there that your demigod dickhead is crossing his *t*'s in, my cosmopolitan cruiser, that car has escorted a lot of very smart people over the years, and a lot of once-were smart people—the once-weres, they are always more eager to talk, to justify, but I listen.

—Ah-ha, so you only know his work by reputation, not by study.

—I know his work by impact. Some people I drive need passage to pleasure, but not everyone. Others need passage to sanctuary.

I recalled his assertion that he had a two-body trunk. The Driver said,

—I listen to them, too.

He shrugged. I said,

—So, if you are talking about complicity, then what about your own complicity? If merely seeing out the duties of his job proves his guilt, then what are you doing in seeing out the duties of your job? Aren't you just being complicit to whatever complicity you imagine he's guilty of?

The Driver laughed and shone the flashlight under his chin, making an oil spill of his features.

—Tonight, he said, I will help in the recovery of the manuscripts. But in the morning, that man isn't going home with them. And you are going to be my accomplice.

As we walked on, I kept my own silence, noble or ignoble I was not sure, but it was what I required at the time. Walking in these conditions demanded my attention. If a mind was not a mind in isolation, but only a mind in thinking, and thinking about something, then my mind was simply the mind of walking, not the mind of listening. I was moving into the world, my foot into nature, rather than the world moving into me, in the form of this man's disturbed thought. (And he was still talking, as we continued to walk parallel to the road, talking about other things now, other things like all the different cats he takes care of, how the town is just cluttered with them, most having been orphaned of their owners and now propagating on their own, how he takes them in and such, but mostly he seemed to be listing their outrageous names to me, and I was doing my best to pay no attention.) The world I was moving through was only and entirely the world I apprehended, as that was the world that came into chafing contact with my body. Sure, there was the world of the numinal, the things beyond what I could see—all those dark unknowns out there—but those things were essentially unapprehended and so they were not of my thinking and even as they infiltrated my imagination I had to remind myself that I was not apprehending those things and so they did not functionally exist as I stomped through this flora, this flora that struck me as surely invasive. (And now the Driver appeared to think I was interested in the territorial disputes between creatures with names like Meatball, Wizard, and, confusingly, Ducky.)

I reminded myself of my work, my real work, the work of making images on paper and—when the rationing of certain useful materials would finally be lifted—on canvas. I reminded myself of the limits of a page: In a still life, the lines that go to the edge end there in both the numinal sense and our sensory sense. That we continue those lines to the edge is merely a gesture, not toward what is beyond that perimeter (and no, I did not care about Wizard's dietary fussiness!), as there is nothing beyond that perimeter, but what is within it; that conceit provides a sensory life to the thing itself, the still life. There is nothing of that still life beyond the page or the canvas, and so there was nothing about the Philosopher's life and work beyond what I perceived. (Really, how could a cat not like milk?) My grandfather's hat, for example; it existed in the frame of the Artist's representation of it. I apprehended it as a representation of an object I know, an object I know that was once owned and worn by a person I did not know, but the fact that the lines of the straw encountered the edge of the canvas, appeared to transgress the frame, that merely created the meaning within the frame, not beyond it. And what of the man who wore the hat?

But maybe I was getting it all wrong. The way tools became an extension of the body when they were out of sight, did not art also become extended beyond our sight? The Philosopher had not yet been able to provide an answer to my question of the hat, if he had any information about my grandfather (and Meatball, to be fair, did sound like a bit of a terror, so I could see how Ducky would simply want to guard his own space), if he'd in fact perished in the conflicts that happened before my birth.

I had now become frustrated with my thoughts, their recalcitrant ways. When starting a charcoal study on a sheet of paper, and seeing it go bent and wrong, the lines refusing to steer toward or reveal a design, one could crumple the paper, throw it into the waste bin, and begin again. But thought did not offer such fresh starts. One could, at best, cuff the side of one's own head, attempt to rattle the mind clear as one would an appliance on the fritz, but that was rarely helpful. So instead, I attempted to ground my thought, locate it outward: That house there, it would make for an appropriate object for one of the Philosopher's heuristic direct descriptions. I'd always found these exercises calming, reassuring. Beginning with how I apprehended the object of study within the general, this was a house, familiar in form and function. Now, seeking to understand the ways in which it particularized itself against the general, I could see that its door was—brown? It was hard to tell in this light, and it was hard to think clearly with the Driver barking instructions at me, as apparently that was the house. The house? The Chemist's house: home of chapter two. We were here!

The Driver said he would wait behind this blueberry bush, which I suspected to be an elderberry bush, and that I would go up to the house, following the Philosopher's instructions. I agreed, my eyes averted from the Driver, and as I trudged toward the moonlit house, I attempted to focus back on my heuristic exercise. The house I was nearing, however, was failing to particularize itself from the genre of *house*. I noticed no features I could see as unique, nothing to notice other than its houseness. Instead, my thoughts were atangle with who, precisely, I was helping obtain the manuscript inside. In getting it from this house—that is, in knocking, introducing myself to the resident, the elderly Chemist whose name and general description the Philosopher had given me, and reassuring him of my trustworthiness by telling him a few details about his relationship with the Philosopher that only a close associate of the Philosopher would know (these details seemed to constellate around the practice of kite-darning and a need for typewriter ribbons and repair), so the Chemist would then feel confident in handing over the pages—I was bringing it back to the Philosopher, but I was also bringing it into the more immediate clutches of the Driver.

At the front door, I knocked. I waited. I knocked again, this time by lifting and smashing down the metal knocker that was fashioned in the shape of a bony hand clutching a rock. Cobwebs stretched over the top of this door that had not been opened in some time. I looked back at the elderberry bush, which, now that I looked at it, might have been a blueberry bush after all, then I turned back to the door. I peered into the window just to the right of the door, saw nothing, no light in what must have been an abandoned house, not an uncommon condition of houses here. I could not aid the Philosopher without it appearing that I was aiding the Driver. Either way, each action—conspiring with the Philosopher or conspiring with the Driver—necessitated the same action: I broke the window.

My hand, which I cut on the window, still smarts, and this attic is not exactly glutted with medical supplies. The wound is on my left hand, on the back, a one-inch exclamation mark in red that in the hours since has become embossed in distressing ways. Concerned about infection, I have torn a strip of fabric from the lining of my shirt and tied it around my hand, only to then worry that such a gesture is pointless. A length of cotton will not ward off infection. If anything, this artifact of my shirt contains more filth than my hand would otherwise encounter, and here I am introducing into my system new vectors of disease.

Beside my own stack of pages is the one I first discovered in this typewriter. *To whom it may concern, if I should be expired upon your reading this, please know—*

If these pages turn out to be my own last will and testament, not due to the vicissitudes of political violence but because of bacterial stowaways making it all the way to my vitals, then I hope someone may find in my words here something that might recommend me well, and I hope, dear reader, that if you're flipping through these pages while my sepsis-felled body is slumped on the floor beside you, you might whisper down to me some of those qualities, as, at the moment, I feel blind to them, as I was to a great many things.

I have now removed the provisional bandage. I have dropped it on the floor beside the typewriting table, and the Chemist's cat is now pawing at it.

Imagining a reader—a reader more discerning than merely my own future self—coming across that ghoulish scene, reading all this, has me looking a bit closer at these words for what they might reveal. And do they reveal the same ghostly trace of deep sky blue that haunted the black typewritten letters of the Philosopher's manuscripts? I see only black words. I hold my hands up near the gas light, look for the dusting of blue. I see, blessedly, nothing. But I have to return these sore hands to their work, to not let my narrating self a moment's rest in his hot pursuit of my narrated self, because when the former finally catches up with the latter, when the past I can control here on the page folds into itself the present and beyond, what a terrifying unconcealment it will surely be. My left hand still hurts.

Inside the Chemist's house, my not-bleeding hand, without my thinking, groped along the walls for a light switch. As soon as it occurred to me that this house, like that of the young man and his perished father, might not operate on electricity, I found a metal knob and turned it. I was relieved to see the light surge on. When the house went from purely tactile and olfactory (musty with the sour hint of almonds) to visual, what I saw in the light (after tending to the small but prolific cut on the back of my left hand, pressing it with my right thumb as firmly as I could) was alarming in its normality: an antechamber mildly festooned with bric-a-brac, a table the width of a small book that had one job and that was to hold a vase for a clutch of flowers that did not exist, the hall ahead hung with little blue paintings, everything dimmed beneath a fuzzy layer of dust. I had the task ahead of me of finding a single butcher-paper-wrapped manuscript in an unfamiliar house whose resident had long since abandoned it, and I would approach this methodically, room by room.

In the first, a kind of salon space with plenty of lush furniture for sitting and socializing, things seemed arranged to emphasize what happened between the chairs and loveseats and couches, not on them. I found a silk napkin on an end table and wrapped it around my wounded hand. On the walls were more blue paintings, larger. I initially mistook them for windows, if windows in the dead of night could look out on a perfectly blue sky, cloudless save for the wisps of brush strokes that revealed the white canvas below. They were all framed in gilt engraved with floral patterns, designs that contrasted the shocking blueness they held. I walked through the salon and into a hallway that connected it to a bathroom and, eventually, a kitchen, and leaning against the walls of the hallway, three and four deep, were more canvases, unframed. Each was painted a blue that was hypnotically blue. From the light coming in from the salon, I only wondered at the vibrancy of the pigment, until I found a hallway lightswitch. I turned it on.

It was unlike any blue I'd been able to touch with my hands before, a deep sky blue that was beyond blue. This blue beyond blue was not the blue of sadness or the blue of sad music, as neither of those was actually blue; nor was this blue the blue of a blue note in the sad blue music, as that was not blue but flat, and this blue was not flat but round, creating a sensation of rolling a smooth pebble of ice over the tongue; nor was this the blue of bluegrass; nor was this the blue of coming out of the blue, or of blue bloods, as those were not blue; writers had called learned women blue and puritanical scolds blue, and yet they also used it for the salacious and crude, and none of those was blue much less this blue—*this* both as the deictic and the emphatic—nor was it the blue of a blue oak or a blue poplar, as those were not blue; nor was it the blue of the blueberries on the blueberry bush outside, as even that was not really blue but purple. It certainly was not the blue of the sea that Homer imagined carrying Odysseus home, as that was not blue at all but wine-dark, since Homer did not have the language for blue, and maybe I was only able to see this blue because I was able to make that little bloom of sound with my mouth; no, the word *blue* was inadequate for this blue that was beyond my language, this blue that could have been the blue of the Blue Nile that was unseen by me; and it could have been the blue of a robin's egg or a peacock's breast or a macaw's nape or a kingfisher's crown, as none of these I have seen; it could have been the lethal blue of a frog in a faraway forest untrod by me, a frog the lightest touch of which would fell the halest of men; it could have been the blue of hyacinth or morning glory, though, again, I could not confirm. I could confirm, though, that this was the blue of Hokusai's wave that appeared to be eating Mount Fuji, the blue of Van Gogh's star-drunk night and the blue of Bellini's extravagantly subdued skies that stole the eye from every foregrounded saint; this was the blue in which Vicente Palmaroli found unsounded depths for the dress of the dullard duchess Maria de los Dolores Collado y Echague; and this was the blue, I suspected, that shaded the shadows beneath my grandfather's hat. That is, if the pigments and chemical processes of mechanical reproduction are to be believed: I had yet to encounter any of these within the proximity to see the mud-ruts of brush strokes, the devastating evidence of an embodied instinct free of the mind.

In the Chemist's kitchen, the walls were not hung with more blue canvases, but the walls were still covered in this blue. It would be inaccurate to say the walls were painted blue, as that implies a coherence and completeness that this lacked; rather, the walls were smeared with it, as if by a child—a child with the use of a ladder, as the chaos of blue crept up the walls to the tin-paneled ceiling. Beyond the kitchen, a study—to guess from the large desk and few bookshelves, the tall wingback armchair facing a fallow fireplace at the far end—and here, the streaks of blue no longer bore the integrity of a brush bristle; now, the streaks were clearly the work of fingers, bare hands dipped in the stuff, clawing angrily at the walls. It was here, though, that the bookshelves—cluttered not with books but with the stuff of experiments, implements and tools that seemed to approach familiarity to me and my experience in artists' workshops, while remaining stubbornly unfamiliar—proved fruitful.

It would be disingenuous to suggest that finding the Philosopher's manuscript was as simple as walking up to one of the bookshelves in this blue-splattered study and picking it up as if it were a book in the library stacks; but the process of my laying bloodied hand on the manuscript was quite tedious and need not be reproduced here, so suffice it to say: I found it.

With the light slightly better in the kitchen, I took the manuscript out of the study and laid it on a wood cutting board. And as with the tedium and time of my finding it, the tedium and time of my reading it need not be rendered here, except that I found the conditions oddly ideal. The light, the standing at the cutting board, the sense of urgency, the lack of readily available Victorian pornography, it all combined to hone my ergonomic and attentive powers on gleaning what I could from the manuscript before returning to the Driver and then to the Philosopher. I was thinking that if the Driver succeeded in relieving the Philosopher of the manuscripts tonight, at the very least I could help in the document's reconstruction.

This chapter—its typewriter ink, like the earlier chapter's, shadowed in that same deep sky blue—was, from what I could hastily gather, a diagnosis of atrocity. From the earlier chapter's attention to the ways that art and art-making were resistant to the problems of rootlessness, this chapter seemed to build an explication of how technology, as a product of that fragmentation, was designed not toward the revelation of external truths, as was the way of art, but rather toward the self-annihilation of the drivers of modernity. Despite the conditions that allowed my focus, I still encountered the same problem I did whenever I first read the Philosopher's work, that of vocabulary. The repetition of words like rootlessness, unworlded, the supratemporal—I understood the words *qua* words, but within the Philosopher's arch syntax, these took on the suggestion of the sinister, something that could not quite be defined explicitly for fear of making it manifest. It was like reading a ghost story, and I could only wonder at what animated the Philosopher's imagination this way. In the past, I'd had the resources of ancillary materials and professors to help bring these terms into focus, but now I had only some wooden spatulas, a few metal whisks, and a stray pestle. I thought of what the Driver had said about silence. From what I'd excitedly gleaned from the earlier chapter, I'd been comforted by the notion of art as the salve against the fragmented world, though I had not understood exactly what he meant by the fragmented. The supratemporal seemed to have something to do with it, a force that was not subject to time and place. And yet the Philosopher's explication of this force was not confined to the abstract realm in which he usually dwelt; this force seemed to be actual individuals. His writing was no longer about a way of Being—be authentic, be the truth-seeker—but about a way of seeing, specifically: seeing the Them. He had previously written about the malevolent force of the Them, but it remained abstracted into all the small compulsions that move you away from your authentic self. Now, the Them seemed not only specific, if unnamed, but embodied. I read on and was relieved to find something graspable and agreeable: *The telos of technology is its own power.* Yes, I thought, considering the ways that, even in my lifetime, the mechanical implements of life had seemed not to reveal anything other than my own dependence on those implements, and the insidious ways that the world I sought to render in my art was not the world I had been given. Whereas the old masters I emulated once saw and presented a world of straw hats, I was fighting to present straw hats in a world that no longer had a need for straw hats, compelled to present a world that existed merely for its own self. But, as soon as I encountered something nice in this manuscript, something I could really get behind, something I could extract, hold up like a little pearl of wisdom free of its gooey shell, the Philosopher went on and had to write that *atrocity is brought about not by the subject enacting it, but by the object that perpetuates the means of it.* In his subject-object construction, the object, then, was both the recipient of the atrocity and somehow the one culpable of it. There was something quesy-making about finally feeling like I understood. I decided, then and there, that I did not much care for comprehension. I much preferred the ways that ambiguity could draw you in as if by vacuum, let you place your own things on its empty shelves and then affirm your tastes as curator.

I flipped ahead to the end of the chapter, hoping that its conclusion would return me to the realm of the abstract—if the world of the concrete was a sidewalk to the face, the world of the abstract was a cloud. *The enacting of atrocity, then, becomes the imperative of the subject, that very necessity rendering the subject guiltless.* I shuffled the pages back into a neat stack, contained. I shuffled myself around the kitchen for a time as if looking for something for a recipe I was not making. I reminded myself, as I clawed through a deep drawer of ladles and tongs (how many does one kitchen really need?), that I really knew nothing of philosophy. I was, had always been, a tourist. I was an artist, after all. Not even that. I was a student. A mere doodler. I'd only come to this man's work for self-serving purposes, none more self-serving than to convince myself that I could even understand it. The spice rack was a mess of the unrefilled and the downright mislabeled. I was here not as a conspirator of the Driver, nor a student of the Philosopher; I was here merely as a functionary, and the stupidest thing I'd done this night was thinking I could think. And that's when I picked up a small jar, sitting stoutly beside the thyme, of white powder. Initially reading the label as *coriander*, I peered closer—inspecting not the label but the contents, as I'd never seen coriander powdered quite so finely—but in doing so *coriander* came into focus as *cyanide*.

When I dropped the jar, it shattered on the tile floor, a cloud puffing out of the mess—which I glimpsed only briefly before running back into the study. Stumbling out of the kitchen, I looked for a door to keep the contaminated air trapped in the kitchen, but all I saw was a red velvet curtain draped between the rooms. This seemed like an oddly porous separation, both in terms of chemical and bacterial aerosols, but also in terms of the class divides one usually associates with such homes. Regardless, I yanked the velvet sheet across the doorway, pinning it to the door frame as if that might prevent the spread of cyanide-dusted air. I retreated back into the study, not taking my eyes off that door, on alert for sight of the poisonous seepage. I put my hands to my chest, a calming measure, only to realize that my hands were empty: I'd left the manuscript in the kitchen where it would sponge up the poison. I had no choice but to go back for it, and I had to move fast before those pulpy pages absorbed any more of that stuff. The silk napkin still bandaged my hand. I unwrapped the silk from my hand and covered my nose and mouth with it. I smelled my still-damp blood in the fine fibers. I approached the velvet curtain from the side, as if about to take an intruder by surprise, then I slipped into the kitchen. I quickly grabbed the manuscript, noting the mess of chalky white cyanide on the floor, and, with the Philosopher's chapter tucked under my arm, I scrambled back out, into the study. I leaned against the desk and caught my breath, only to realize I was drawing huge gulps of air from the pages of the manuscript I now clutched to my chest. I took some assurance in the dimly grasped knowledge that whereas arsenic could take years to kill me, cyanide's effects would be instantaneous; it was, after all, the anticipation of death that was most excruciating.

I set the manuscript on the desk, which was more formidable than I'd first noticed. It was long and deep, running along a windowless wall, and I'd initially taken it to be a desk not because of its form but because it held, along the back, a series of reams of papers, all propped vertically in metal dividers. This was clearly a place of work. Further down, the splatter of blue paint became more gratuitous beneath a cluttering of the following: a few glass beakers that were wide enough to fit my fists (I'd initially thought they were beer glasses), metal funnels, a few inch-deep metal pans, glass stirrers, rubber droppers, clumps of steel wool, a bottle of aspirin, a bottle of muriatic acid, and another bottle of what I now knew not to misread as coriander, sealed. Spread out like a placemat was a fine cheesecloth stained with a blue sun that darkened into a pigment my eyes could not distinguish from black at its very center. Beside this was a flat metal scraper, its blade covered with clumpy blue, frostinglike.

The Chemist, it seemed, had been rendering—from a stash of cyanide, perspicacity, and a robust disregard for safety—his own Prussian blue. There had been a shortage of the pigment since I'd entered university, its primary ingredient in demand elsewhere. My professors lamented the dullness of Prussian blue's neighbors on the color wheel. If, as Goethe wrote, "we love to contemplate blue, not because it advances to us, but because it draws us after it," then my mentors bemoaned the lack of reticence in the blues left to us, the cobalts and azures. A good color, my professor had told me, does not just lie there. (I wished he had stopped there, with what I understood, but he continued, saying that a good color demands that you put in the work if you're going to fuck it.) The first person to synthesize Prussian blue was an occultist who did so by way of experiments on dismembered animals (a tale occasionally invoked by that professor of mine who bemoaned both the dearth of Prussian blue and the glut of feral dogs). Then a chemist, in the days when chemistry had not yet crawled out from under the spooky aegis of alchemy, concretized the process with cyanide, but only after poisoning countless children with an arsenic-laced emerald green that was quite popular in its day for nursery room walls; Napoleon's fondness for it eventually liquified his organs in Corsica. That color theory class I took my first year of university was also a history-by-footnote of horrific death. I wondered now what this man, the Chemist, had in mind when he took a considerable amount of state-supplied poison and processed it here on his wooden desk (and did not people like this have places to do such things?) into a blue beyond blue, if his intent was to reconcile the primal forces of beauty and death, or if he was just profoundly bored here in his mountain estate.

A cat—*the* cat—jumped up onto the desk. My instinct was to prevent him from knocking over the glass beakers, but he lingered on the far end, away from the mess of instruments. The cat remained Buddhic in his composure. He was clearly domesticated, owned by the Chemist and abandoned here in the house, so it occurred to me that I could bring this lovely little creature—small, ginger, rather jellicle in his bearing—back to the Driver, activate that man's nurturing instincts, maybe distract him from his other intentions. I reached out to pet the cat and he immediately sprung from the desk and into the wingback armchair. I turned and, facing the front of the chair for the first time, saw that the cat was now resting on the lap of the Chemist.

The Chemist appeared fantastically old, and I could not yet be sure if he was sleeping or dead, but he did not stir when I let out a series of curses I did not know I knew. He was so shriveled in his pose that no part of his body had been visible from behind the wingback chair. His face, a rictus of permanent distaste for the world, suggested death, but the way the cat nuzzled into his lap suggested sleep, still retaining the warmth of life. I stepped back, felt the edge of the desk behind me. The Chemist was wearing a smoking jacket over silk pajama pants that concluded oddly in a pair of wingtip shoes. The fireplace that he was angled toward was drafty, let in a breeze that rippled his sparse mustache hairs. I figured I should leave him be, just get the manuscript, and maybe the cat, and let him enjoy his sleep or death. With the manuscript tucked tightly under my arm, I gestured toward the cat. I fluttered my fingers and clicked my tongue at him. The cat looked at me, lowered his head to the Chemist's lap, then jumped to the floor. I crouched down and let him smell my hand, then I rubbed his head. Soon, I was able to pick him up with my free hand, a cat under one arm, some philosophy under the other. In my periphery above, I noticed movement, something so slight it might have been imagined.

But then I looked up and saw: The Chemist was awake. He looked at me with cloudy eyes, his mouth agape. In a moment, two things happened: I rose from my crouch and the Chemist let out a gasp of—what sounded to me like—fear. I began to say something, something reassuring to cover for my obvious theft, but he was frantically searching through the pockets of his smoking jacket. I thought he might be looking for something to help him communicate, a pad of paper if he had trouble speaking, or some sort of amplification device if he had trouble hearing. I explained that I was an associate of the Philosopher, reciting the details the Philosopher had coached me to recite, the details that would convince the Chemist that I was to be trusted, but the old man was too busy in his pockets to listen. I said,

—I'm a friend.

And in that moment, he finally pulled what appeared to be a small metal-and-glass capsule from his pocket and put it in his mouth. It was instantaneous. The carotid arteries went taut under his chin, yanked as if by noose.

I am of two minds on what happened next, as I now have two competing memories of what must have been concurrent events: I recall running away, and yet I have unshakable images in my mind of what then happened to the Chemist's body. With cat and manuscript tucked to my torso, I ran across the study, not toward the kitchen but into a hallway that circumnavigated the kitchen back to the antechamber. The Chemist's jaw meanwhile was clenching shut with vise-like intensity, jaw muscles flexing the sides of his pale patchy skull, his lips curling up, only briefly exposing his teeth as his mouth was quickly filling with a foaming something. Running down the hill, toward the patch of blueberry bushes, I vaulted over the minor juts of rocks and ropey roots, until the Driver emerged with his flashlight. Meanwhile, the Chemist's body, not his mouth but his body, was letting out a gasp as it was seizing, like a fist clenching, all his skin going from red to purple in an instant. The Driver, seeing my urgency, helped guide me back to the road and once we were there, he made sure to shine the flashlight before me as we again traversed the underbrush just parallel to the potentially explosive road, and he asked me why I was holding a cat. Meanwhile, behind us, the Chemist's body must have been squeezing itself out like a sausage casing.

I attempted to explain the cat to the Driver, but I'm not sure my words were coming out in a manner or sequence that allowed the Driver to understand. The cat was using my shirt front as a scratching post, and its warm body against my skin made me realize just how cold I was. I'd given my coat to the Driver back when he'd thought it possible to clean the gore from the automobile's hood and windshield. Now that I'd properly stolen two items from the Chemist's house, if returning the manuscript to its author can really be said to be stealing, I regretted not taking the extra moment—before the Chemist had bitten down on the cyanide capsule that triggered complete bodily implosion—to get a new wool coat for myself. Much of these thoughts were coming out in fragments, comprehendible to me only in how the Driver was attempting to repeat what I was saying back to me, his effort to puzzle out what I was saying. Walking along in the little glow of the flashlight's beam, that little meter-wide spotlight that contained only a step or two at a time, everything beyond my current action was out of sight: I was only responsible for this one single action of placing one foot down, then another after it. No room for anything else. I did not care to make myself understood to the Driver. The cat curled tighter against me and only faintly bore the scent of bitter almonds in his fur. The Driver and I fell into a silence, and the rhythm of our steps took on the quality of a large cow slowly chewing its cud.

Before passing back through the border checkpoint, the Driver steered me back onto the road and walked close beside me, whispering to me to just follow his lead. As we passed through, the Driver simply exchanged a wave with the soldier, who remembered us, did not need to check our papers again and was briefly charmed by the cat. The soldier made a puckered face and instructed us to wait here. I was too exhausted to be nervous, and, as it turned out, there was no need. He just rooted around in his little booth until he found a cube of cheese, which he fed to the cat.

Not long after moving through the checkpoint, we neared the Driver's sedan. While I waited on the side of the road, the Driver trudged through the line of trees behind which the Philosopher had been waiting for us in the blood-covered automobile. The cat's eyes reflected light I could not see. I heard a door slam. I saw the Driver's flashlight dart between the trees, the automobile illuminated in shards. The Driver shouted,

—He's gone!

I must interrupt the chronology here to quickly document this conversation that is coming up through the attic vent. This began just a moment ago with two voices clenched in angry whispers. Although I know these must be the Driver and his Compeer, I am not quite able to identify which is which, primarily because I have not previously heard them speak this way, this way that has the timbre of a vaudeville mustache-twirler in devious aside to an implicated audience. Monologuing in tandem, the two voices are hard for me to differentiate:

—Something something was not part of the plan.

—Listen, a plan is a floor, not a ceiling, a support, not a constraint. Something something have achieved the plan, and now we have a new plan.

—But this is not one of those trials.

—But it is.

—We have the something something. That is the thing.

—But he can still wield influence. That is also the thing.

Listening to this, attempting to transcribe this, I think I can now parse the difference between the men, my ears having adjusted to this new tonal language. The Driver is a bit more croaky, the Compeer nasal, with vowels that seem shaped at the front of the mouth.

—Something something on their way to being rehabilitated, the Compeer says.

—He is not a foot soldier, the Driver says. If we facilitate something something we are complicit.

—I do not want another something something.

I am aware that things of great consequence are being deliberated below me, but I find the act of recording them to be diverting enough. Which is to say: When focusing exclusively on the act of transcribing, I mercifully have no room left to cerebrate. I become a passive vessel. It's not so much that the typewriter becomes the ready-at-hand extension of my toiling body, but that I become the ready-at-hand extension of this conversation, a thoughtless, agentless body. But, of course, I have, I see, diverted myself from that task by reflecting on that task and in such diversion have alienated myself from the very thing I was just doing.

The cat seems more engaged with the deliberation below. He is now at the floor vent, pawing at the sounds, swiping them, claws out. I must not be the passive vessel of transcription; I must be the cat: actively engaging with the language, the meaning, the import.

But the voices are now gone, the dialogue having ended with the punctuation of a door closing. The cat is still examining the breezy wraiths emerging from the vent, trying to identify any words they might contain. But it's all silence now. Just the two of us breathing at a slightly accelerated pace—the cat because of the excitement of his little game there, and myself because of whatever military-grade amphetamine that was ticuntured into my tea. The relief of spending my alarming energy thoughtlessly transcribing the first-floor debate is now being replaced by the dread of having to reflect on what came next—that is: what comes next—but as that past tense gallops closer to the present, I anticipate the promised unconcealment, something satisfying like folding a flat sheet, edges meeting, geometry creating containment. So: onward, or rather backward, to that empty automobile, to that time we lost our Philosopher.

There was nothing in the back seat: no suitcase, no manuscript, and certainly no Philosopher. I let the cat into the automobile, placed the second chapter in the back seat, and then searched more thoroughly, as if a man of late middle-age could have tucked himself beneath the aluminum cover of the console's ashtray (in which I found only two cigarette butts, nosing up like hopeful sproutlings from the earth).

I closed the door and ran out to the road. I first ran down the center of the road, thinking the Philosopher must have been on foot not far ahead. I imagined approaching him from behind (I could surely outrun the man; his gait had suggested he was quite infirm) and tackling him moments before he set foot on a landmine's detonator sticking nipple-like up from the gravel. But that scenario reminded me not of my heroic potential but that I was also at risk of getting blown up, so I swerved back and forth, as if the landmines were actively taking aim at me like archers from towers posted on either side of this dark country road. While the Driver was calling after me, asking just what I thought I was doing, calling me names derisive of my intelligence, I began expanding the scope of my search: into the bushes at the base of the trees (the Philosopher peering out like a nocturnal critter with his spectacles reflecting light, of which there was little save for the Driver's flashlight behind me) and then into the branches above (the Philosopher clinging up there, tweed limbs tight to the trunk). It all seemed perfectly plausible, that I could find the Philosopher out here on a dark road, if I just scrambled fast enough. It all seemed perfectly plausible, until I ran face-first into a tree.

What I thought was a concussion turned out to be (though a concussion might still be lingering) the Driver's flashlight in my face. He shouted,

—What is going on in that head of yours? Have you gone completely mad?

I generously thought that his volume (which was considerable) was meant to pull me from the depths of brain injury, not to express anger. Either way, though, it hurt my ears some. He threw the flashlight beside my head and grabbed me under the arms, hoisting me up to a sit.

—Now, listen. If I'm going to continue to risk my car and my person out here, I need to know you're not going to hop off like some galvanized toad. Don't worry, we'll find him. It occurred to me that he might have begun to get suspicious of our intentions and made a run for it.

—*Our* intentions?

—Yes. Because you're my accomplice now. As I was saying, I worried for a moment that he might have fled, but that was just worry. After all, he only has the one chapter. You've got the second. And he still needs us to get the third. Whatever his reasons for leaving that car, whether they were inspired or delusional, by will or by force—

—By force?

Calming me with a hand to the chest, the Driver said,

—It's a possibility that we need to entertain. No matter the circumstances of our losing him, he can be only temporarily lost. After all, where is he going to go?

I attempted to get some saliva back on my tongue to explain my ideas about where, be it bush or tree, he might have found hiding, but before I could, the Driver continued:

—More importantly, where are we going to go? We're not going to go searching up and down this road in the dead of night, not with these explosives hiding about. And we're not going to just drive home with the car in that condition, and we're too far to walk. And I'm not going to just camp out for the night. Not when I can get us to the Madam's in less than an hour. There, we can get a rest on some soft cushions, a wash-off for the car, a wash-off for us, too, and a warm cup of something. And we can get there without crossing any regional borders.

It was then that the pain in my face announced itself, first subtly, then extravagantly. The idea of going somewhere that promised some comfort was appealing, as I had already sustained a series of minor injuries—to say nothing of having witnessed two grotesque deaths. But I had some concerns. I asked,

—In driving to the Madam's, might we not get exploded?

He shook his head. He looked behind me and pointed into the darkness. He said,

—New road not far up the way, straight to the Madam's. She arranged it for delivery of foodstuffs and such. Cut the path not more than a month ago. No reason for it to be rigged.

He patted me vigorously on the shoulder.

—At dawn, we can head out and find him. There are a few places around here that take boarders. He probably wound up at one of them, but it'll be best for us to find out in the morning. Two men approaching in the dead of night does not always garner the kind of hospitality we're hoping for. Yes?

Without thinking, I began telling him how I'd seen the Chemist die. I was suddenly talking about how I'd woken the old man up and he'd been scared and put the capsule in his mouth and bit down, about how it had looked like he'd just had his breath taken away, like he was struck by some beautiful sight, only his breath never came back. The Driver nodded.

—Cyanide cuts off cells from taking in oxygen, letting oxygen out. Total organ collapse occurs pretty quickly.

I asked him how he knew that (where had such a man gained such knowledge of the body and the particulars of the violence we do to it, and how many men had he poisoned into complete organ collapse, as Nero's attendant personally saw to the cyanidic demise of the emperor's family after they'd been deemed state enemies?). The Driver looked up into the cool night, all aclutter with stars.

—I read it in a science magazine, he said.

I nodded. I got myself to my feet. I agreed to go with him to the Madam's, to leave the Philosopher out in the dark until morning.

The time it took to drive to the Madam's was enough to get us twice that distance. The new road the Driver had spoken of had clearly not been designed for automobiles. The Driver said that due to the unique demands of sundry-delivery at the moment, the road mainly hosted horses pulling carts, but, judging from the finesse required to steer between trees, it seemed more equipped for mongooses dragging bushels. I commented such to the Driver, but he did not respond. He was more focused on the driving, very concerned as he was to not damage the undercarriage of his cosmopolitan cruiser. The dried blood and whatnot on the windshield also posed added difficulty. After turning around a tree, which might have actually been multiple trees grown twisted into each other, we came into a clearing—more than a clearing, it was a small field. At the far end was a sizable farmhouse lit from within. If I'd come across this estate on my own, I would have guessed it to be nothing more than a farm whose livestock had trotted off in the confusion of these last few years (not uncommon, from what I've gathered; my aunt spoke often of cows that would come sniffing around her door), but with the Driver I knew better of what to expect inside.

The Driver did not park out front. He pulled into the small barn just to the side of the house. We got out of the automobile, and instead of walking with me back toward the house, the Driver began looking around on the deep shelves that lined one wall of the barn. From there, he pulled two metal buckets. I asked if we were going to go in, but he just shooed me on and said he'd clean this mess first, but that I should head on in, that the Madam would see to me, to just say that I was with him. I hesitated, then followed him as he walked out to a small well pump just outside the barn. I offered to wait for him, and he laughed, said the Madam didn't bite.

As he filled up the two buckets, I turned queasily to the house. The windows were draped with white doily curtains, through which I could only make out occasional passing shadows. I (eventually) approached the front door. Was there a secret knock? A password I needed to whisper through the crack in the door? It only occurred to me to worry about such things after I'd knocked. I'd given one polite rap on the wood, but now, thinking about a secret knock, I added a few more raps that had a clandestine rhythm. The door swung open and a woman in a green garment that seemed to be both robe and dress said,

—What's the fuss, Gene Krupa?

This sounded like a prompt for a secret password. I looked over to the well pump, but the Driver had gone back into the barn. I began to explain to the woman whose hair was done up in a bandana that I had come with the Driver, but before I could get even there I was sidetracked by explaining that I'd seen someone blow up, and she very quickly began shushing me and guiding me into her parlor. I'm not sure how much I told her as I walked from her front door to the chaise lounge beneath an odalisque that appeared to be depicting a woman on this very chaise lounge, but this woman—the Madam, I assumed—did not seem to care enough to pay attention. The chaise lounge, being neither chair nor sofa nor bed, presented choices I was not prepared for, choices of body and propriety, and I found myself mimicking the woman in the odalisque above me, as if the image were more instructive than decorative. But I discovered that this slightly supine pose was quite relaxing.

The Madam, sitting across from me on a chair that was entirely obscured by her flowy garment, asked me how I was doing. It seemed an odd question, as if we'd known each other and were catching up after a long interval, but for some reason, after feeling a sudden and frantic need to tell her so many things when I was at the door, now that I was sitting down and catching my breath, I said, simply, that I was just fine. She asked me if I wanted some tea, and, suddenly recalling the tea I'd been offered by the young man who was now being scrubbed off the hood of a stately automobile, I declined. She asked me my name and where I was from, all the kind of nicely sociable things I too-often forgot, and I found that stating these basics of myself was oddly calming, as if I were not just telling these things to her but to myself. As I had so often followed the Philosopher's models and performed (both to myself and in my art) heuristic direct descriptions of the objects that constitute experience (here is a house), I now approximated that process with myself (here is a person). She took a slow breath, then asked,

—So, what are you in the mood for?

I'm not the simpleton others have taken me for. I knew what she was asking. Nor am I the milquetoast others have taken me for. I knew this was the opportunity I'd been looking for, that if I was going to be sidetracked from my primary mission of the night it might as well be toward my tertiary mission of the night. I said to the Madam,

—My aunt would very much like it if I experienced sexual congress before returning to her.

The Madam seemed taken aback by this, touching her fingers to her bare neck as if she had pearls to clutch. I saw the need to elaborate:

—For the posterity, of course.

She hesitated before offering a smile. She said,

—Yes, of course. Well, you know in these difficult times maintaining a modest home like mine takes more than just gumption and elbow grease. It's really the generosity of my gentlemen visitors that helps keep the gas in our lamps and the kick in our steps.

Her cheeks were deeply dimpled. I explained to her that I had no money, that I was merely a university student. I was prepared to leave. I understood that I'd initiated a transaction without first securing my end of that contract. I would slink away in shame and go help the Driver scrub the person-bits from his cosmopolitan cruiser. But before I could get up from the chaise lounge (not a simple task), she said,

—Oh, a student. It's been ages since we have had a student here. It's a relief to know there are still schools out there. I suppose I should have guessed that you weren't a soldier.

She gestured toward my body, or my general presence.

—Tell me, what do you study?

It occurred to me that she was no longer in the mode of professional hospitality; she was genuinely curious. I told her I make art. Her smile changed into something soft, less effortful.

—Well, we all make art. But not all of us choose media that befit a classroom. So, Student, you must have chosen—

She stood up. She walked over to me. She kneeled beside me. She picked up my hand. Her hand was warm and soft. She examined my fingers, one at a time.

—Whatever it is, it does not leave a trace. You're clearly not a sculptor, not with these nailbeds. I see no ink or paint.

—I focus on charcoals, still lifes.

She placed my hand back on my knee. She looked up at me and said,

—Charcoals are for studies, not the real thing.

—I'm just a student. I'm not yet the real thing. Besides, materials are hard to come by these days. Charcoal is easy to find.

She stood up, her face above mine now. She nodded at the painting above me, the odalisque.

—The man who painted that, he was a very famous artist. Perhaps you can recognize him from his brushstrokes.

I turned, craned my head up to see. The scalloping texture of the foreground, the feathery dry-brush technique of the velvet, the complex fan-brushing of the draping silks in the background—I had no idea who the artist was, but I gave a name with confidence. She sighed and said,

—To be honest, it might have been. I can't actually recall his name, though he did assure me he was famous—famous in certain circles.

She pulled a cigarette from her pocket, walked over and lit it in the gas lamp of a wall sconce. She pointed the cigarette back at the painting.

—Surely, you can recognize her, though.

I looked back at the painting, squinted at the heavy-lidded expression of the woman. I angled my head in a way that made clear to the Madam that I was not staring at the exposed bosom. Since my earlier guess of the artist seemed to get a passing grade on the sole force of my assertion, I tried that again and said, with a bark of certainty that surprised even me:

—Eleanor of Aquitaine!

This seemed to charm the Madam more than convince her of my aptitude. She took a slow drag of her cigarette, then said,

—Close. That's me. Maybe you'd say that *was* me, but it's still me.

—Yes, of course! How true that time atomizes the self. We are all the Ship of Theseus!

I had not, however, noticed that this was her. Paying such close attention to the specific techniques of paint patterns on the canvas had somehow obscured for me who that paint depicted. I sat upright on the chaise lounge, my body no longer able to ape the posture of the woman in the painting. The Madam said,

—When he was my guest, he couldn't afford to be generous with his money, but he could be generous with his talent.

She was standing closer to me now. She pointed from the painting to me, a soft warm puff of ash falling from her cigarette to my cheek.

—I could use something new to hang around here, but I don't much care for still lifes. Surely you can do figure?

I waited in a second-floor bedroom that neighbored a room that was audibly in use. The Madam had already brought in a coffee tin full of pencils as thick as my thumb and dried fountain pens, a mostly empty inkwell, and a stack of drafting paper of various sizes, but said she had a really nice eight-by-ten frame, so ideally I should do something to fit that. She'd mumbled to herself that a gilt frame needs a brunette, that a blonde in there would be too much yellowness, and now she was off to find a live figure for me, someone who would also take care of the act of remittance, details of which we would discuss after the portrait. After poking through the coffee tin, which was on the cocktail cart she'd rolled into the room, I went to the window, doily-draped, and looked out at the barn. Rivulets of water and whatnot were running out the open door, though from this angle I couldn't see in. I sat down on the bed, which was centered in the room. It was a wide bed, perfectly square in fact, so that without the nightstands to orient me, I might not have known which end was the head and which the foot. Sitting there, I noticed, with some horror, my own feet. I'd tracked a fair amount of dirt into the bedroom. I quickly removed my shoes, and, failing to find a proper shoe rack, I scooted them under the bed. Then I went about looking for a hand broom and dustpan with which to clean up my footprints. Failing again to find any, I used my socked foot to sweep what I could of the mess into a neat pile at what I'd determined to be the foot of the bed. I rehearsed in my head what it was that I had said I would do. All the particulars. I shuffled through the paper the Madam had brought me, mostly tablet tear-outs more fit for a typewriter than a figure drawing. I realized that I was having trouble keeping the paper still; slight tremors in my hands were animating anything I held. Surely I was just anxious about having left the Philosopher out in the cold until morning. I found that if I held one shaking hand in the other shaking hand, the two could wrestle each other still.

So I was clutching my hands as if in tight-fisted prayer when the door opened and in walked a young woman in an ill-fitting nightgown. She had to hold her shoulders rigidly up in order to keep the neckline decently high on her chest. She looked at me, closing the door softly behind her, and I thought of Edgar Degas's brothel monotypes, those sketches of all those submissive women in sad states of undress, their eyes averted, gazes oblique, as if unable to look back at the artist looking at them. This young woman seemed to be looking not quite into my eyes but around my eyes; she was clearly the demure maiden who would need to be coaxed from her coyness by the reassurances of an experienced portraitist.

—Why the fuck's your face all fucked up? she said.

I immediately averted my eyes, drew a hand to my cheek. To the rug beneath my feet, I explained that I'd sustained a few minor scrapes this evening.

—I'll say. You look like you had your face runned over by one of those things what goes rolling over the ground—what are those things?

—Tanks?

—You're welcome!

She broke out in a laugh that I imagined showed the rural teeth of a woman unseen by a dental professional, but in truth I was still looking down at the floor.

—D'you get the joke? I got it in a movie. Been waiting for just the right time to try it out myself.

I focused on selecting a pencil from the coffee tin. The activity in the neighboring room was becoming ecstatic. She said,

—But with all sincerity, it's a good thing I'm the one gonna be in this picture.

She took a seat on a tall stool, her legs spread, nightgown falling between.

—Now how's this? Or should I go full naked? I always thought that if a picture makes a man stiff, then it's smut, not art. I want this to be art. Maybe I could go full naked but cover certain bits with my hands.

I told her that just as she was would do fine. With a sheet of eight-by-ten on a small wooden board propped on my lap, I found that focusing on the familiar task helped steady my hands. Identifying the center of gravity was a good starting point, as from there I could ensure that the limbs were all angled appropriately. Once those angles were set, I spent some time on the foreshortening of the left leg. The body was something unfamiliar to me, but it was essentially a collection of geometric shapes—cylinders, balls, blocks—and geometric shapes were predictable, certain in the ways they interacted with space and light.

—So, what, you don't go to the movies?

In fact, I did not.

—I used to go to the movies all the time. Best one is this one where a guy gets sweet on a blind girl so he pretends to be rich. Guys who come through here think I'm blind like that girl. Think they can pretend they're something else and I won't notice.

A shoulder was a sphere.

—Except this one fella come through here last week, wasn't trying to put on airs, said he'd come from the efforts out in P——, had a chunk of wall all blue he'd pulled out of there, said it'd seen more death than he'd be able to imagine, little round chunk of wall, blue like an eye.

A foot was just a foot-size rectangle.

—He tried paying with that, I said no thank you. But I can get behind this kind of thing. Art. Best part of the movie, though, the guy, the bum, he falls asleep on the lap of this statue, you know like a statue like Victory or Justice as a person, this dirty guy all lousy on a porcelain lap. You do statues? You look like you like statues.

Shading on this paper—too glossy—was proving a challenge.

—If you're gonna draw me, you should look at me, huh?

I looked at her as much as I needed to for my task, though the young woman did not seem to think it was sufficient.

—It's okay, she said. Lots of guys come through here and have seen things that mess them up. This one guy couldn't look me in the face or nothing. It's okay. I'm sure he probably saw lots of things, like death and stuff, all right in his face.

I told her that I, too, had seen horrors. I paused to sharpen my pencil with a dull blade from the coffee tin, whittling a new point. I told her I'd seen the ravages of poison on a man's body right before my eyes. I told her I'd seen a man get blown to smithereens, saw him splatter all over my vehicle.

—Oh, God, she said. That's disgusting.

I heard her shift.

—Oh, shit. Sorry. I should be still, huh. Like you can't paint a moving target.

She seemed to shift back to approximate her original pose. I was tending to a splintering pencil tip. She said,

—Oh, but that was heartless of me, to say that, about a moving target, what with what you've seen.

I told her it was just fine with me, that encounters with death were nothing to be afraid of. After all, I explained, the deaths of others were always secondary to one's own, as they were instructive to one's understanding of one's own death. And it was in considering the lessons the deaths of others had for our conception of our own death that we as individuals could finally move away from the insidious influence of everyday fellowship with others, the They. She said,

—That is the biggest pile of horse manure I have ever heard.

Looking up from my sketch, I saw a young woman whose jaw was askew with revulsion.

—You think when my dad died when I was eight, I was there taking notes on what the tuberculosis did to his body so I could be ready for when it gets me?

—Well, that isn't precisely what—

—Those are the thoughts of a goddamn lunatic! When you see someone die, you see someone die. You see them shit themselves. You know who sees someone die and instead can only think of themselves? Egoists. Crazy people. Dangerous people.

—Please remain as still as possible for the portrait. The shadow on your forearm is tricky.

—And, what, it's good to only see your own stupid self in someone who is about to go the way of all flesh—because it frees you from other people? My God, man, you've got to be a real fruitbat to go thinking that sort of thing. You're too bent for even a straitjacket. Leave you out with the loons and they'll flock away.

—Once again, please try to contain your movements, for the sake of the portrait.

—I mean, really. A brain that thinks thoughts like that is a brain that can't figure the difference between a cunt and belly button and then feels flattered by the tight fit. I mean, really, that's some real egoist delusion-type tripe.

Finished—I announced that I was finished with the sketch! I set down the pencil with more force than I realized, causing the young woman to startle a bit on the stool. She clapped her hands under her chin.

—Oh! Can I see it?

I said of course. She hopped off the stool, and as she came around to see my work, she was no longer taking care to keep her neckline above her nippleline. Standing beside me, her face next to mine, she breathed deeply, taking in the portrait I'd made of her. She placed her hand on my hand, my dominant hand that brought graphite to paper, and she patted my fingers.

—Well, she said, that looks nothing like me.

—It's not a photograph. It is art.

—But art shouldn't look like a pile of cans and some wiggly noodles.

—You were moving quite a bit during your sitting.

—You were too afraid to even look up at me. Maybe if my limbs looked like crunched aluminum you'd have been more interested in looking my way.

Paraphrasing for her the Philosopher's *Towards a Complete Aesthetics*, I told her that art was a deconcealing of truth.

—Are you saying that in truth I'm a rubbish bin full of broken toys and cow teeth? Because that's what that looks like to me.

I reminded her of my academic credentials. She sighed and picked up the sketch.

—Well, I'll see what the Madam says.

She took my work out into the hall, closing the door behind her. I tried to put my flustered attempt out of my mind. My hand had been unsteady; perhaps I had a concussion from the tree, after all. It was no debit to my reputation; no one in this building would set foot in the art world I was apprenticing to enter. I'd earned what I'd earned, so I set my thoughts on what I'd earned. I put my shoes back on. That seemed proper. Then I sat on the edge of the bed, the sounds of carnality filling my mind, sounds that soon revealed themselves to actually be filling the neighboring room, not my mind after all. The young woman came back into the room, still holding her portrait. She flapped it down on the nightstand and said,

—The Madam said it's not full-service worthy, but that I should still make sure you're taken care of.

The particular way the young woman took care of me, as I sat there on the edge of the bed, was more akin to a protracted but quite pleasant handshake than what I was expecting, and this did not seem like it would produce the results my aunt had hoped for. I asked if the young woman could call me some of those things she'd called me earlier—to drown out the sound from our neighbor, I clarified. She did so, though with less enthusiasm or creativity as she had before. I closed my eyes. Just beyond her voice, I heard that of another. It was the voice of the Philosopher, like the wise ghost of Hamlet's father imploring the young Wittenberg student to become a man of action, encouraging me, it seemed, to return to the path of my mission, beseeching me, his voice so intimate in my ear that it almost seemed as if he were not whispering from the spiritual plane of the ether but rather from the proximity of the neighboring room, shouting,

—Sit on it!

I'm interrupted again by the sounds of new arrivals at the Compeer's house. Engines outside, doors closing—that unique rubbery and suctiony sound made only by automobile doors—and feet crunching gravel. Lots of harrumphing, back slapping. I'm nervous to peer out the window for fear of being backlit by the gas lamp, these new strangers seeing a shadow puppet of curiosity in the mansard window.

But, hold on. I have returned. I was quite careful with how I positioned my head vis-à-vis the light and window, and so I think I was able to spy the doings down there undetected. It looked like this: two motorcars, black or at least dark enough to be taken for black in this light, newly arranged in the roundabout, plus another vehicle, unmarked by any military affiliation but with the build of something made for rough terrain. By the time I periscoped one eye above the window frame, the fellows who'd arrived in those vehicles were no longer visible outside but were audible downstairs. I can hear them now, and my co-author is repositioning at the floor vent. These conversations, though, do not come strangled by whispers. These conversations are full-throated, noisy even. Unfortunately, despite the clarity of the words making their way through the attic vent, none of them seems worthy of taking down here. Even the cat has removed himself from the vent. These people—I am guessing they number no more than seven or eight—seem more interested in vulgar prattle than in the whisperings of conspiracy. I hear the clink of libation, smell the earthy musk of tobacco.

I am conscious of not wanting to move my chair too much, for fear that it will reveal my presence. But of course that's silly. It's no secret that I am here, even if they have not called for me to join them. And what if they did? Might I enjoy the puff of a friendly pipe, the sociability of peers? Of course!

Since smashing that exclamation mark to the page, I have left and returned (and there it is, that space between paragraphs, the *now* of which I am in pursuit—or not quite the *now*, but close, as this writing seems to be like the curve of an asymptote, aching for contact with the present moment, its disclosure, its unconcealment, never to touch).

This is what I have returned from: not quite sociability, or at least not the kind I had hoped for. When I came downstairs, they greeted me boisterously, these men in dungarees and suspenders, shoelessly putting their feet on pieces of furniture that are not ottomans, and the Driver quickly gave a survey of my contributions to their mission, exaggerating some bits, underplaying others, and the group of men without ties proceeded not with inquiries about my own origins or interests or hobbies but with a story that I seemed to have interrupted, a story that I will not add to these pages, these pages that, even though they already host images of horrendous gore and now the ribaldry of my actions with the young woman of the Madam's employ, certainly do not need to be sullied with such a sailor-tale as that. Anyway, I believe these men are preparing for violence, but, regardless, back to the bordello.

Hearing the Philosopher clearly shouting in the neighboring room, I rushed out before the young woman had completed her task. In the hallway, which was a long corridor of about a half-dozen doors, a bedroom presumably behind each (hopefully at least one door led to a water closet, though), I found what must have been the correct door. I placed my ear to the door and heard the Philosopher saying,

—I am not done! Where are you going?

Could it really have been him, though? Maybe that was the voice of another man of a certain age whose timbre was both throaty and adenoidal.

The door suddenly opened and a woman of alarming height and dizzying red curls burst out. Behind her, I caught a brief glimpse of the Philosopher himself. He was standing in the middle of a four-poster bed, holding on to the wooden canopy, as the mattress beneath his feet seemed infirm. Idly bouncing on the squeaky springs, he was quite nude and quite sweaty. The hairy flesh of his torso appeared loose like an oversized shirt even while what asserted itself below was taut. It was unclear if, in that brief moment before the tall woman shut the door behind herself, he saw me, as he could have just been watching her leave. With the door freshly slammed, the tall woman shouted back through the door,

—You pay for time, not experience! And the time is up! I do not care if you feel unsatisfied. You pay for time, not experience!

But if the Philosopher had taught us anything it was that time and experience were inextricable! The tall woman looked down at me.

—You know that guy?

Didn't everybody?

—Tell him to clear out. It's not a hotel. Someone else is going to need that room.

She turned and walked away, down the hallway toward the stairs. As I turned back to the door, I heard some heavy and cumbersome item of furniture scraping the floor on the other side. I called to the Philosopher, excited for the final leg of our journey, excited to tell him how I'd recovered his second chapter and a cat, but mostly just excited that we'd been reunited, that he was safe and not lost in the woods. I opened the door. It slammed into what must have been a dresser, only a centimeter between door and door frame. The Philosopher had barricaded himself in the room. I put my face to the crack but saw nothing aside from a thin, unrevealing strip of room. I let him know it was me, let him know that I was here to help him. He called out,

—You can help me by bringing me a brunette.

All of this—the sight of the Philosopher in his unadorned shame, his bizarre demands—was starting to affect my equilibrium like a rollercoaster. I simply could not align the man who'd written about the self with such supple and subtle delicacy with this man who was now explaining that he had not achieved orgasm and so he deserved service until satisfaction was achieved. I told him that I had secured the second chapter and that—

The chapter, the manuscript: Where was it? With a cold flash, I realized I'd left it in the automobile; the Driver was with the automobile and had made it quite clear that he was not to be trusted with the Philosopher's papers. I had no reason to think that the Driver had absconded with the manuscript, not yet (he seemed to be, like the Philosopher, a completist, wanting the entire three-chapter tome), but I couldn't just leave him with it unattended. I did not compound this error by revealing it to the Philosopher.

I told him the mission had gone splendidly and that after securing the second chapter, we had only one more stop to make, so if he just put his trousers on and came out of there we could get going. This grabbed the Philosopher's attention; I could hear the shift in his voice as he asked how the Chemist was getting on these days. My throat was quite dry when I said that he was doing quite well and that he sent his regards. So, I asked through the crack in the door, did he want to put his trousers on and resume our evening's journey? He was silent a moment, and just as I thought I heard the jangle of a buckle, a voice bellowed behind me:

—We got a dawdler in there?

I turned to see the Madam. She was holding a wooden baton, about the length of my forearm, leashed to her wrist with a leather strap. She rapped it against the door three times. When the Philosopher did not respond, the Madam looked at me and said,

—I hear you know this gentleman?

I told her I was his associate, that the Driver and I had been chaperoning him this evening. At the Driver's name, she nodded, mumbled something about him always bringing in riffraff. I told her that we'd been separated from the Philosopher and had been searching unrelentingly for him.

—Unrelentingly, huh.

Then she looked down, said,

—Put your pecker away.

As I did so, she said,

—New girl brought him in. Found him on the side of the road, confused.

Then she shouted through the door:

—Sir, if you would like companionship for an additional hour, we can take your donation.

To me, *sotto voce*, she asked if he'd barricaded the door, and I nodded. She tightened her grip on the baton. Finally, the Philosopher said,

—I do not have any more money with me.

The Madam told him he'd have to leave then. His voice less certain, he said,

—But I would like to see another woman, please. Preferably one with brown hair and rounder in the hips than the previous—

The Madam banged the baton against the door and shouted that he had one minute to collect his effects and clear out of the room. I shouted through the crack in the door:

—We just have one more stop to make! We have almost all the manuscripts! Sir! Please put on your pants!

I said these and other such things, but it was too late. The minute was already up. The Madam was scooting me away. She braced her shoulder against the door, gripped the doorknob with one hand and the baton with the other. She grunted and pushed. I could hear the dresser scrape against the floor. When the door was open just wide enough for me, but not the Madam, she told me to squeeze through and move the dresser out of the way. I saw this as a chance to intercede, and the door scraped my ribs as I snuck into the room.

But when I was through, I didn't bother helping with the dresser. I was in the room. And the Philosopher wasn't. It didn't make sense. This wasn't the back seat of a sedan, though; there were plenty of hiding spots. So I looked under the bed, no Philosopher, in the wardrobe, no Philosopher, behind the folding pingfeng, no Philosopher. I considered that he might have leapt out the window, but it seemed to have been painted shut. His clothes, trousers included, were still folded on a seatback, so wherever he was, he was still in full shame. How could a man whose life's work was about the absoluteness of Being keep evaporating into non-Being? And that—while the Madam was shouting at me from the hallway to move this fucking dresser already—was when I gazed into the yawning maw of the laundry chute.

I rushed back to the dresser and was able to slide it the rest of the way from the door. Before the Madam could process the scene through the syllogism that I had just used—that (first, the major premise) the Philosopher was no longer in the room, and (second, the minor premise) the laundry chute was the only viable means of escape, therefore (the conclusion) the man must have thrown his body down the chute—I rushed past her, out into the hallway and toward the stairs. It would only be a matter of moments before she could deduce, as I had, that there was a nude man down in her linen room, so I had to get there as fast as I could.

This involved taking two and three stairs per stride, a haste I was not accustomed to, and when I saw the tall red-haired woman appear at the foot of the stairs, I got tangled in my steps and grabbed the banister as if it were a lifeboat. I managed to prevent myself from falling, though not from appearing as if I were engaging carnally with the banister. The tall woman told me to simmer down, and I asked her as calmly as I could where the linen room was, that it was very important, on orders from the Madam, and she pointed down the hall, under the stairs. I barreled down the hall and found the one door that seemed uninviting enough to be purely utilitarian, and sure enough it was the linen room.

A row of scrubbing boards, coppers, and mangles lined one side of the room, large canvas-lined hampers along another, and ironing boards were folded up beside linen closets. Directly across from the door, just over one hamper, was the egress of the laundry chute. Rushing over, I hoped to find the naked Philosopher curled like a baby in the hamper, the fall through the chute having placed him gently down as if by the loving hands of a parent. But: it was empty. He was already gone.

I ran back through the first floor of the Madam's, passing by her various employees, now loitering around the parlor, and I emerged out a side door. Across a small patch of dirt was the barn. Maybe the Philosopher had found his way back to the cosmopolitan cruiser.

In the barn, peering through the sedan's windows, I saw that he had not. I was struck, however, by just how clean and unbloodied the automobile was. The Driver must have done some admirable work, especially since, while driving through the cold night air, the blood and whatnot had seemed to have congealed into something gummy. Here, though, the cosmopolitan cruiser, in the glow of the single lightbulb hanging down from the ceiling of the barn, looked showroom ready. To my relief, I spotted the manuscript of chapter two still there in the back seat, as yet unstolen by the Driver.

Walking out of the barn, rounding the corner to the front of the house, I spotted, on the porch, talking in the light of the open door, the Madam and the Driver. She seemed distressed, angry, scolding the Driver in both a yell and a whisper. I slunk back around the corner. It occurred to me that if I could just find the Philosopher, the two of us might be able to drive off with the manuscripts, leaving behind the Driver and his plans for sabotage. But the Philosopher eluded my pursuit.

Then I heard it: a meowing, not that of the Philosopher but that of a tag-along cat. I backed away from the house, craning my neck up to see where the meowing was coming from. Tucked beside a second-story dormer window, the naked Philosopher was crouched with the Chemist's cat curled on his lap. The Philosopher's grip on the cat seemed less out of affection and more for the warmth the animal's body provided. In the moonlight, the sight—the Philosopher's hirsute body indistinct from that of the cat—had a cryptozoological quality to it, as someone else might have mistaken this for a creature of myth, a werecat, perched gargoyle-like above a roof abutment, about to feast on the villagers below. But I knew better. This man was harmless, and he needed me.

I tried to get the Philosopher's attention, but not wanting to draw the eyes of the Driver and the Madam just around the corner, I couldn't make much noise. I looked around the barn for a ladder but found none. My darting about the house earlier had given me a confident knowledge of its floor plan, which meant I was able to ascertain, within a certain margin of error, which second-story room the Philosopher and the cat were crouched outside of. My only option in rescuing him was to go back through the house and help him in through that window. He'd surely be surprised and delighted when I threw open those shutters.

So I went back through the side door, up the stairs and down the second-floor hallway where I came to what must have been the correct door. It was closed, so I let myself in and was halfway across the room before I realized it was in use. When I politely acknowledged the people otherwise engaged on the bed—the man flopping atop her like a fish on a very tolerant boat deck—the sight pulled my gaze, and it wasn't until the man screamed that I got back to the real goal, rescuing a great man of letters who was tragically being warmed only by the clutch of a tabby, and I opened the window and began folding myself through it. The people behind me were now launching objects my way, and I received first a shoe, then a small vase on my backside, which did not hurt, but it did hurry me along.

Once outside, I found the roof to be much steeper than I'd anticipated. My leather-soled shoes failed to grip the shingles, and I slipped. Soon, I was face-down, holding the ledge of the window with both hands, my body draped over the roof abutment, my feet dangling off the edge. I looked up at the window and saw a decorative cigarette lighter—one of those tabletop numbers that could also serve as a paper weight—fly out. It sailed over me and hit the wall of the barn. The Philosopher, whom I now saw was crouched with the cat just beside the frame of the dormer window, reached over and closed the window. With one hand on the cat, he extended the other hand toward me, and I imagined he was about to pull me up, but instead he gestured flappingly and said,

—Come on now. Get yourself up here.

I did get myself up there, and soon the three of us, the Philosopher, the cat, and I, were hunched in the crook between the dormer window and the roof. The Philosopher did not seem surprised, nor delighted, to have me appear at his rooftop hideout, where he was nude save for the cat, all lousy on a porcelain lap. But I needed him to understand a few things: First, that we'd now successfully regained possession of two of his three chapters, and with minimal death. Second, that the Driver was not to be trusted, about which I did not go into detail (I did not, frankly, have the temperment to explain to this man that people bore such cruel opinions of him and his work). And third, that it was imperative that we get his trousers back on so that we could hurry away—without the Driver, if possible—to get the final chapter. But the Philosopher wasn't paying me much attention. He was focusing on the cat, who was purring. I realized that I could feel the vibration of the purr, as we were all huddled together in the wedge of the roof, so any movement was felt by all. The convulsions I now felt weren't from the cat; they were from the Philosopher. He was crying. He hadn't been looking down at the cat; he'd been looking down to hide his tears. He said,

—I wanted one more.

—One more, yes. We only have one more manuscript to recover.

—I wanted one more of those women, and the mean one didn't give me another.

—Sir, we really need to get off this roof and be on our way.

—I told her I didn't want a tall one, and she was so mean she gave me a tall one.

I realized, then, as the cat was becoming irritated by the tears and nose-matter dripping down, that I had not planned a way to get off the roof. I asked the Philosopher,

—Don't you want to go get the rest of your book?

I looked around, hoping that the roof would somewhere slope down to offer easy access to a balcony or porch. I said,

—We must get it, so it can go into the world and be a great, beautiful thing.

He stroked the cat's head. That was when the Philosopher's odor hit me, an oniony sweat. He sniffled, wiped his nose with the back of his hand, and said,

—Rilke said that the beautiful is nothing but the beginning of the terrible.

Thinking he was being self-critical, I consoled him by saying he could revise the terrible parts and make them beautiful.

—Hölderlin said the beautiful can unite extremes of intimacy.

I did not know what he was referring to. He said,

—I just wanted a breast to suckle.

I realized then that we shared something in common; both of us, apparently, had suffered an interruptus.

—But now, he continued, they despise me, those women in there. I don't much like being despised. I'm not accustomed to it. I shouldn't have to be.

His eyes were dry now; he was staring at something just beyond the cat. His skin was clammy; I felt his muscles clenching for warmth. I recognized that Rilke now, that Hölderlin; he'd cited them in *Towards a Complete Aesthetics*. I said,

—This may not be the ideal moment, but I'm wondering if I could ask about *A Straw Hat*. You wrote that it was painted in the north of M——. I have good reason to believe that it might have been my grandfather's hat. I'm wondering if you could tell me more about—

But he interrupted to voice further frustrations with the Madam's denial of his requests. The weeping despair of a moment ago had given way to teeth-clenching rage. I attempted to calm him with my hand on the confusing musculature of his upper arm. I told him I wanted to help him get the rest of the manuscript, but that first we needed to get down from here and get him clothed.

And just like that, as if summoned by my words, the top of a ladder slammed against the edge of the roof. This was enough of a rattle to silence us, and we huddled there listening to the sound of someone's weight moving from rung to rung, the top of the ladder shifting with each step, and soon the Driver's head appeared, and appeared quite angry. The Philosopher and I clutched tighter to each other, like siblings caught in the midst of some foolishness. The Driver leveled a few curses at us, questioning our intelligence, criticizing our behavior, especially at this, his place of employment. I expected the Philosopher to fire back in indignancy. How dare the Driver, a mere hireling of the Philosopher's, speak to us, or at least the Philosopher, in such scolding terms! But the Philosopher cowered, averted his eyes, his face in a rictus. This, the Driver continued, was his place of employment. He'd brought us here, and we'd brought him shame. The Driver commanded us to come down immediately. The Philosopher cleared his throat to ask if he might have a robe. The Driver looked down to the ground and asked if a robe might be provided. The voice of the Madam came up from below:

—He crawled out there bare-balled, he can crawl down bare-balled!

The Driver forcefully gestured for us to get on the ladder, then he climbed back down. The Philosopher called after him, asking if he could just go back through the window. Again, the Madam's voice came up to us:

—That's one of my girl's workspaces! You've already encroached upon her, and now you want to encroach again? No more encroaching, Mr. Encroacher! Now crawl down here like the little racoon you are!

The cat leapt from the Philosopher's lap to perch on the peak of the dormer window. It was a clear, decisive move. Of course the cat would stay here, where he would receive the kind of care that neither I nor the Philosopher would be able or willing to offer. I scooted cautiously to the ladder first and began to make my way down. The Philosopher, without first waiting for me to get to the ground, began to descend above me. The cat meowed after us. I looked up, thinking I would get a last look at the Chemist's cat in the moment he became the Madam's cat; I'd smile my farewell, but when I looked up, instead of the cat's warmly cool gaze, I saw only the dark scrotal underside of the Philosopher, his anus like the aphoristic abyss that is said to, when stared into, stare back. I stumbled on one of the ladder rungs, and in the brief moment before catching myself wondered if my last vision of the world, before falling to potential death below, would be the esteemed, though curiously fascinating, perineum of ontological discourse.

When we were both safely on the ground, we stood before the Madam. The Philosopher cupped himself and put his eyes to the ground. While the Driver was removing the ladder to the barn and then starting up the automobile, the Madam offered further censure to both me and the Philosopher. She then tossed the Philosopher's effects—his crumpled clothes, but also the manuscript of his first chapter, still bound in butcher paper— onto the ground before us. I could have helped him, but instead I watched him gather up his things, his body bent and shaky. The Driver pulled out of the barn, the automobile gleaming. He leaned across the bench seat, opened the passenger-side door, and said,

—Get in, turkeys.

I got into the back seat, and as the Philosopher was attempting to get into the passenger seat, the Madam gave him a light spank on his bare, slightly deflated-looking backside; this startled him, causing him to drop his clothes and manuscript. He took a flustered, muttering minute to again gather his things from the dirt, during which the Driver leaned back from the front seat and said to me in a low whisper,

—One more manuscript, but two more stops. When we leave the next house, it is imperative that all three manuscripts are in that case.

He nodded to the portmanteau at my feet.

—And that it is in your possession. Do you understand?

I don't believe I gave a verbal or gestural response, but just as the Philosopher was finally getting himself and his things into the passenger seat, the Driver said to me,

—Good.

Reader, you must know that the cat did not become the Madam's cat, that he is perched here, my surly co-author. And I understand that knowledge of this might have drained that above farewell of the appropriate sorrow, but please understand: At that moment I was genuinely sad to part with the patchy orange tabby. That discrepancy—between the feelings of me-past and the knowledge of me-now—shows there is still a ways to go before the former meets the latter, though I can hear his footfalls. My co-author, however, hears no such thing, and continues to rove the edges of our writing quarters, sniffing out evidence of creatures past. The cat's curiosity about this space has already illuminated it for me in different ways. When I was first shown this attic, I saw only the furniture it contained: minimal and functional, a spare collection of tools for me to get through to morning. But as I objectivize the space through the eyes of this cat, the floor has begun to take on nuances of woodgrain, webbings of plaster cracks, and warps of baseboard that were invisible to me just an hour ago (though even typing that word, *hour*, gives me the vertiginous feeling that shadows any attempt to discern time this night). The ways in which the cat is alive to the possibilities of this space is both wondrous and devastating—the former for the eddies of awe that swirl in the smallest detail, the latter for the realization that those are ultimately opaque to me. The cat takes a break from the hallucinatory poetry of space, and returns, hesitantly, to the vent in the floor.

The visitors are still below us, but their conversation has calmed, from the roiling boil of their prurient blather to the simmer of something more conspiratorial. The cat isn't swatting at the ribbony vowels that are coming up from the vent, just sniffing. I, too, would like to know what they are discussing. I could go downstairs again—they were, last time, encouraging me to stay, after all; it was my own decision to remove myself. I have played my role, but I am not myself one of the conspirators. It always seemed that apostating would reveal a new schema, but I have none. This seems somehow unfair. I have, though, a cat. The cat continues to prowl the perimeter of our shared space. He disappears into patches untouched by the lamplight, sits there until I wonder if he's abandoned me, found some unseen egress and escaped my company, but then he begins finding new dust motes to engage, new forms of play. His perception economizes nothing; every detail of the world is equally deserving of both his disinterest and his devotion, depending on the vagaries of the moment. A moment. I must review my progress to this point. When I last left the musky interior of the Driver's automobile, back on that previous page, it was rumbling along, on its way to its penultimate stop.

Since the Philosopher was having great difficulty getting dressed while in the passenger seat of a moving automobile, the Driver pulled to the side of the road. There, the Philosopher was able to stand up and properly get himself back into his clothing. This took longer than expected. When we were all three dressed and seated and mobile again—appearing, in our newly cleaned automobile, as nothing more suspicious than three nocturnal motorists out for a country drive—the Driver said,

—So I'm going to need you to clarify what we can expect at this stop. Considering what we've encountered at the previous stops, I think it's only reasonable for us to be able to assess levels of risk.

The Philosopher seemed to have a different bearing now that he was dressed; the slouching, sobbing man crouching unclothed on the roof had been replaced by someone fit for a dais lectern, transformed as if merely by costume change. He said that the woman who was housing his final manuscript had been his student many years ago:

—Before everything became so complicated. She was a brilliant student. Stubborn, but endlessly curious. She once stood up in class and accused me of minimizing Bergson's durational model of time. She was wrong, of course, but you do not often encounter such boldness. She'd so surprised me that I was unsure what to say.

I asked him how he responded, and he said,

—Well, I forbade her from speaking in class. She was permitted to only speak to me in private.

The Driver asked, in terms rather vulgar, if he then coited her. The Philosopher refused to respond to that question, though in refusing he did offer the Driver a conspiratorial regard that had been denied me up on the roof. The suitcase was next to me on the back seat. In it were two of the three manuscripts we were to recover. I ran my finger over its latch. The Philosopher continued,

—She did not complete her degree. She should have. Instead, she married. We maintained a correspondence, even as her marriage took her abroad. She wrote about parts of the world that I had only ever known through dime novels, places I'd thought imaginary, but in her words I had to regard them seriously. She described for me a species of moth that when resting on a delicate branch could be mistaken for an orchid. To this day, when I see an orchid, I stare long enough to see if its petals twitch, if it could take flight.

I slid my hand under the suitcase, clandestinely assessed the weight of the gradually filling valise. It was good to feel a solid heft to it.

—But her letters stopped.

The Driver interrupted to point out that we'd be at the next border checkpoint soon, and that the Philosopher should get into the trunk for the crossing. The Philosopher seemed a bit perturbed by this interruption, as if he were about to scold the Driver for insolence, but he did not. When the automobile stopped, he opened the door and got out. The Driver and I got out, too. I realized this time that I did not need to get out of the automobile. The Driver needed to get out because he needed to unlock the trunk. The Philosopher needed to get out because he needed to get in the trunk. I, however, only needed to get out of the automobile because I wanted to get out of the automobile. It was, perhaps, my sudden awareness of my superfluity that caused me to exaggerate my own utility to this somewhat simple and by now familiar activity: As the Philosopher was easing himself sidelong into the trunk, I lifted his legs, making a show of how secure his feet were with my guidance over the threshold. The Philosopher swatted my hand away as if it were a mosquito.

The Driver and I returned to our seats, mine in the back with the suitcase, and we crossed the next regional border with relative ease. The soldier who asked for our papers did not examine them long enough to even read our names, and he assured us—per my query—that we need not be concerned about landmines beyond this point. When we'd driven far enough past the checkpoint, the Driver came to a stop again, but before getting out to unlock the trunk, he turned in his seat to look at me. He did not say anything, so I opened my mouth to speak, though to speak what I was not yet sure. But the Driver put his finger forcefully to his lips. I remained quiet. He pointed behind me, toward the trunk, then he pointed to his ears. I nodded. I understood that the Philosopher could hear us. Then the Driver pointed to the suitcase beside me. My hand was not touching the suitcase, but the two inches of space between my hand and the suitcase felt charged, the object on the other side of the tiny, massive gulf cathected. The Driver nodded. A lifetime of reflexively mirroring the gestures of others urged me to nod in response, but I knew I was not prepared to do that, so I had to clench down on those impulses, remain still.

The Driver broke his gaze and exited the automobile. When he closed the door, I exhaled, realizing only then that I'd been holding my breath while his eyes were on me. This time, I remained in the back seat. I looked down at my lap, the suitcase animating my peripheral vision, but I did not, despite the pull of the object, look at it.

The Driver and the Philosopher got back in. The Driver steered the automobile back into the road. He confirmed with the Philosopher that we were now close to the final house. The trees illuminated in the twin headlamps reached farther over the road, creating an evergreen tunnel for us to move through. I worried again about the possibility of explosion but took solace in the assurances of the soldier. Instead, I asked the Philosopher why his former student had stopped writing letters. He said,

—I do not know. She eventually became—no longer married. But the damage from that marriage was permanent.

I asked why.

—When I corresponded with her about the possibility of housing the manuscript, reinitiating communication after so many years, her letters were terse, factual. Gone were the flights into the world, flights only her mind, equipped with her language, could possibly navigate. She simply accepted the package that my wife delivered her, offering in exchange, from what my wife told me, no salutation or invitation. So to answer your question, he said, looking at the Driver, I do not know the risk.

I said I would go with the Philosopher. We were now parked at the base of a hill, a path wending up to a cottage. The cottage was backlit by the moon, that brightly dull spy's eye, and the cottage's roof seemed overlarge for its frame. This was common to some of the older homes around these parts, so much effort put into the headwear that not much material was left for what was beneath it. The Philosopher got out of the front seat. I opened the back door, and before standing up I took hold of the suitcase. The Driver reached back and touched my arm. I said I should take the suitcase with me, into the cottage. The Driver asked, ostensibly to me but looking sideways at the Philosopher, if it wasn't better, safer, to keep it in the car. I said it would be safer to keep all three manuscripts together. The Driver's expression as he looked at me was a mismatch: His mouth appeared as a smile while his eyes did something I could not name. He said,

—Are you sure?

I turned to the Philosopher, who was standing just outside the automobile, and asked him if he didn't think it best for me to bring the suitcase with us, but he seemed to be busy rehearsing his reintroduction to his former student. Into the middle distance, varying the emphasis with each repetition, he kept saying,

—It is so good to see you.

I turned back to the Driver and said,

—I will take this.

The Driver—clearly unsure what to make of me and my intentions, just as I was unsure of what to make of myself and my intentions—said,

—All right, then.

I got out, holding the suitcase. I felt the two bundled manuscripts shift inside. By the time I closed the door, avoiding the Driver's eyes, the Philosopher was already on his way up the hill. He was still rehearsing his lines, his voice disappearing as he made it to the stone-lined path. I hurried to catch up, careful with the suitcase so as to not shuffle the pages inside. When I was abreast with the Philosopher, I took the opportunity to continue a previous conversation.

—The farmer wears the hat in the field, I said.

The Philosopher grunted with each step. I continued:

—Only there is it what it is. Equipmentally, it is a shield of the sun, a caul between man and nature: a technology. And yet, the more the hat is itself in-being, the less the farmer is aware of it. The farmer, meanwhile, only becomes aware of the hat, not when it is in-being upon his head, but when it falls to the ground, as it is here, returning to the earth as pure potentiality. And yet, it is only in the painting that we notice these things, both the hat and the animating attention of the wearer. And yet—

The Philosopher said,

—Why are you saying this to me? I'm trying to think.

—But that is you thinking. That is your writing, your thinking, that which I have just recited to you. That was from *Towards a Complete Aesthetics*, the passage on *A Straw Hat*.

—I know that. I also know that I did not write it as a dramatic monologue to be performed *dans en théâtre plein air*.

I told him that in that essay—*monograph*, he corrected me (and as such, I have made that correction to this document). I continued:

—In that monograph, you wrote that *A Straw Hat* was painted in the north of M—— in 19——. My grandfather was a tiller in the north of M—— in 19——.

The Philosopher was now saying, to an imaginary person before him,

—It is so good to see you. You are looking well.

But I continued:

—It is well within the parameters of reason for me to suggest that this hat was my grandfather's. I have his hat. It is in my aunt's home. It must be the same.

The hill was steeper than I'd thought, the path up to the cottage longer. I asked,

—How might you have continued that sentence? *And yet*—? You clearly had great knowledge of how the painting came to be, and the painting is clearly of my grandfather's hat.

—Your hair looks lovely. You have not aged a day.

—I never met him, I said. And it's looking increasingly like his name will end with me. I don't even know how he died. I always assumed it was in that war, the other one. But.

—I'm most sorry to bother you at this late hour, he rehearsed. I hope I did not disturb your husband or other such person?

—But you clearly knew so much. *And yet*—. How did that sentence end? What can you tell me about him? I must—

—Do shut up! the Philosopher shouted.

He had stopped quite suddenly, only a few meters from the hilltop cottage. He was now facing me squarely, his spittle misting my face.

—Shut up! Shut up! Shut up!

His gesticulations were so unpredictable that I had to step back for fear of getting swatted.

—I know nothing of this man, and you know nothing of me or my writings! How dare you read me and think I'm speaking to you, speaking of some common laborer sifting through shit in a field! I did not write about a farmer but about the *idea* of a farmer. If you want a hug from grandpa, don't go looking for it in my work, you daft little shitling!

I clutched the handle of the suitcase with both hands. I steadied my feet on the ground. I attempted to wet my dry mouth. And that was when the lights in the cottage windows turned on. From inside, I heard a woman shout,

—Who is shouting on my doorstep at the witching hour?

The Philosopher gasped, then said under his breath,

—Oh, no, no, no.

To me, he whispered,

—This is your fault!

Then he ran up to the door, now sufficiently lit, and hurriedly straightened his jacket front.

His former student was suddenly in the doorway, her arms hugging her midsection, in a fur coat that she had thrown on over a nightgown. The Philosopher said,

—This is not how I planned to greet you.

Having just opened the door, and having just been so rudely awoken, she was clenching her face against the light inside, while trying to squint into the darkness outside.

—Please accept my apology, he said.

She stepped to the side, as if she were merely a door herself, and the Philosopher walked in. I followed.

Along one wall, pots sat atop a brick stove beside a fireplace, and in the middle of the room a small wooden table had gathered around it a few chairs. What I initially took to be a davenport along the other side of the room was actually a wooden bench covered with many wool blankets. There was a rich, loamy funk in the air, a feeling like worms might nose through the walls, and their reception here would not be an inhospitable one.

It was, at the moment, still unclear how to classify the reception that the Philosopher and I were receiving. His former student had let us in, but she was now shuffling across the room in her very comprehensive fur coat (bear?) without as much as a glimpse up at either of us. The Philosopher stood beside the table and chairs; his posture was hunched, but he seemed reluctant to sit. I followed his lead and remained standing. His former student kneeled beside a belted travel case against the wall, opened it with much unbuckling, and pulled from it a now familiar-looking package. She sat the heavy manuscript, wrapped in butcher paper, on the table. She then waved it away as if it were a fly, sat herself in one of the chairs, let out a sigh, and said,

—Take it, take it.

The Philosopher stepped forward to place his hand on the manuscript, but he did not pick it up. He looked at her. She shrugged. She was old not in wrinkles but in mien, her awareness of gravity and time fully embodied. He said,

—I was hoping to know how you have been. You look lovely.

—I look like shit.

—You haven't aged a day.

—Well, I know that. But I look like shit because I was just woken up in the middle of the night by a man screaming at a child on my doorstep.

This seemed like an apt moment to introduce myself, my association with the Philosopher, and my mature age, but the Philosopher cut me off, saying,

—It was such a difficult hike up that hill. I could sure use a rest and maybe a glass of water.

His former student sighed, lightly kicked the chair across from her, then pointed to the jug beside the stove. The Philosopher shuffled over to the ceramic jug, found a wooden cup beside it and filled it halfway with water that, at least in this light, had a tint that suggested the well water was a bit too rich in nitrogen. As he was helping himself to that, I attempted to sidle up to the table and the manuscript. I began to introduce myself to the Philosopher's former student, and as soon as I got to the part about being his esteemed associate, I placed my hand on the manuscript. But just then, the Philosopher returned to the table with his brown water and shooed me away so he could sit across from her. Back in my corner, I watched the Philosopher sip his water politely, and she regarded him as if he were a small but harmless rodent that had wandered into her home. He said,

—I take it you are no longer married.

In an attempt to join the conversation, I said,

—Divorce or death?

But neither acknowledged me. She nodded to the Philosopher and said yes. Then she said,

—You still have your typist, of course.

The Philosopher asked what she meant, and she pointed to the manuscript. He said,

—I've never been good with typewriting.

—Not that hard. One letter at a time, one word at a time. It's just like writing. Just like thinking. Put one in front of the other.

She jabbed her finger at an imaginary typewriter.

—Just takes practice. Practice and a reason to do it in the first place. You never had a reason to take the time to figure the machine out, I suppose. You always had one of us to do it.

He set his water down on the table, on top of the manuscript. He leaned forward and said,

—You were the best.

Nervous about a possible spill on the manuscript, I moved toward the table, reached toward the cup. I imagined I could make like I was simply removing the cup, but in doing so remove the manuscript to my possession. When my hand was within a finger's grasp of that little still life, though, the Philosopher, seemingly oblivious to my presence, reached back to the cup. Our hands collided, the cup wobbling between us, my heart seizing at the vision of the water washing away all those blue-black words underneath. The Philosopher grabbed the cup, turned to me and said,

—Get your own. It's unsanitary to share use of a water cup.

I again retreated to my corner, and that's when, in my anxious garment-straightening, I noticed my shirt's breast pocket had been sewn shut, a new curiosity for me to nervously pick at. The Philosopher's former student, who had not yet, as far as I could tell, made eye contact with me, said to the Philosopher,

—I wouldn't let you get away with the things your wife lets you get away with. Your impulses are still toward the needlessly abstruse, and I don't mean that old saw about complex ideas being presented complexly. I mean that you still can't keep straight restrictive and nonrestrictive clauses, which just muddles so many things. And she lets you get away with that sloppiness. Still, though, it's fun to see where she's at least attempted to rein you in. Or at least put a nice ribbon on your bellicosity.

—That means you read it?

—I did.

—I have always cherished your input. Tell me. What do you think?

—What do I think? I think of when I met you. I think of that often. There was restlessness in you. You seemed incapable of succumbing to dogma. Physically repelled by it, as if an encounter with the dogmatic was an encounter with the grotesque. In your *Of Man* lectures, you seemed to move as if trying to expel it from your body, the act of lecturing an act of exorcism. Afterwards, I fully expected to glance at the copy of Hobbes on the lectern and see the pages blank, your exegesis so complete that you had excised the words themselves. It was infectious. More than that. It was galvanizing, made it feel like there was a war that needed to be fought and we were the only ones equipped to fight it. We would follow you into battle. We would be champions of Being, too long forgotten, situated in the self that had too long been obliterated as a mere mechanic of reason. That anything could be the subject of this meant that the battle was everywhere. My perception of a hammer became the site of something radical, the way the light hit the umbrella outside a café, our embodiment of the space around us suddenly liberatory. A simple mood now had meaning, contained a truth, was no longer a pathology but an unconcealing of something vital. The lure of that was so powerful, I ignored things. Or rather, the lure had an eclipsing quality, totalizing. I did not ignore things. Things were obscured. Sure, like your marriage, like the fact that my own work had to wait while I finished the edits on yours. But there were other things. I think of how you taught me to cut an onion. Most remarkable thing. Cutting an onion is fascinating. It is an act most simple, an act that has been performed countless times for centuries, using the most basic of technologies. A blade. A hand. And yet it is an act that has furiously resisted mastery. There is simply no way to cut an onion with the perfect grace that one can master any other devoir of the domestic. The carpenter using the hammer holds the hammer and swings the hammer and forgets the hammer is there as it becomes a ready-at-hand extension of his body, the act beautiful—erotic, even—in how body and technology merge, the body sensing the space of the technology, the self expanding. The cook, though, cutting an onion, he can never ignore a thing. It draws all the attention, demands it. You've written about all these simple acts of the banal, elevated them to acts of divination, unconcealment. But you've never written about the cutting of an onion. It's a shame. I think about you teaching me to cut an onion. You had a system, you said. You had, it seemed, discovered the one method of cutting an onion that had eluded people all this time, and in this way the act would become embodied like it never had been before. Brilliant. Except you chopped the tip of your wee finger off, and nearly stabbed me in the tit. The onion was now covered in blood. And I needed the onion. And it was the only one we had. And so I made it work. I wasn't sure if you were so upset because you'd reduced your wee finger into an even wee-er finger, or because your little method didn't work out, or because you now had to eat bloodied onion. Whichever way. The onion, by the way, caramelized quicker that way. So there's that. And I think about my husband. You never bothered to meet him, but he was a great man. Not one of you. He took me far away from here, but your war had to bring him back. I think of the things he saw that I cannot possibly imagine. We slept in separate beds because he began convulsing in his sleep. And I think about that and I think about this. This new thing that is really an old thing. I see the thing that was always there. The anti-dogma was just its own kind of dogma all along, wasn't it. Just depends on what you think the dogma is. What's most infuriating isn't that I didn't see it. I guess I did see it. What's most infuriating isn't that I turned away from it. I did do that, though. What's most infuriating isn't even how you didn't have the courage to say the things you so clearly believe, that you hid behind the requirements of your post. What's most infuriating is just how banal it all is. The evils you see, the dogma you imagine you challenge. It's all the boogeymen of the brutes, their mindless mythology of the wicked and the pure. It's all so stupid. All this shit and it's the stupidest, most puerile lies that got you. You broke my heart. Do you remember my last letter? I made a simple request of you. Resign the rectorship. If what you had claimed was true, if your fealty to the brutes was merely a requirement of your post, then do what so many of us did, had to do. And leave. Here, I'd thought, was what you'd been warning of, the pressures of the They to compel you away from the authentic. Surely, you would understand that. Surely, you would be able to say no to them. But you chose to stay. You chose to stay and watch their butchery and say okay. For years, I fooled myself into thinking that you were back here in unbearable conflict. Forced into the unimaginable. But, of course, you were quite comfortable. You had found your authentic self. And all these men, these starched-collar brutes, your colleagues, they're now choosing the self-slaughter of their little pills, and that's so easy, a simple exit, when I had to pull my husband's hand away as he fought to get his pistol to his temple. He was stronger than me by an elephant's worth, and I had to fight him every day, wrestle him on the floor, when he sought to snuff himself out, when those visions, when that knowledge couldn't be erased. You will never know what it's like to hit a man you love until he is unconscious, just to keep him alive, to tie him to a chair, to keep his hands from self-murder—every day, and then, one day, to fail. Because he saw the things that you shrugged permissively at. You broke my heart.

I interrupt again—or rather, I've been interrupted again: A moment ago, a man entered my writing attic. This was one of the men who arrived earlier, who'd been audience to my visit downstairs. This man was on the larger side, fingers so tumescent they looked like they couldn't close into a fist, and his facial hair had different levels of unshaveness like striations in sandstone. He seemed alarmed to burst into the room and find only me: hunched at this little typewriting table. He entered cautiously, squinting at me, as if at any moment my blurry figure might transform into what he was looking for:

—Commode? he said.

I shook my head. Then he pointed to the bedpan beside the cot, the bedpan that I was at pains to not mention in my earlier inventory of this room.

—That yours?

I explained that, yes, I have been using it (that tea seems to have been quite the diuretic), but—as he made his way to it, his clenched gait suggesting urgent need—I explained further that it was quite unseemly to share such a utility, and that there was surely a proper flushable toilet downstairs. He paid me no regard and voided his blatter into my bowl. I averted my eyes. Buttoning himself, he said,

—You're the student.

I made some noises of agreement, and soon he was standing above me, pointing a thick finger to this stack of pages beside the typewriter.

—This it?

I asked him to clarify his question.

—The papers you got from him?

He flicked this page with his dirty finger.

I explained that, no, the Philosopher's manuscripts were now in the possession of the Driver and the Compeer, and this was merely my own record-keeping.

—You're the one who got them papers, huh?

I said I was.

—Why'd you do it? I mean, I'm glad. You did the right thing. But why?

My eyes searched for the cat where the lamplit floor erased into darkness. Because, I told him, at the moment it did not feel like a decision. There was no longer an either/or.

The man walked away from my table. I noticed droplets on the floor beside the bedpan. He reached into a shadowed spot in that corner over there and picked the cat up, as if materializing the creature from nothingness. The cat curled immediately into the crook of his arm. I realized I had barely held the cat, that I had socialized with him in a largely touchless way. I almost asked if I could hold him, but by now the man was walking over to the window, where he soon gazed idly into the night. I watched the cat watch the man watch the night. And then the man saw something in the night, and the cat saw something in the man, and I saw something in the cat, and we all seemed to tense as if by some sort of electrical current conducted between our gazes. The man dropped the cat, and the cat darted away, and the man cursed and ran away from the window, back to the door, and in his sudden dash kicked the bedpan, which jostled with our shared water, and then he was gone, his heavy boots pounding down the stairs.

Leaping over the spill on the floor, I went to the window and saw: there in the distance, just at the edge of where the house light scoops out the night, a lone figure running arthritically away. Men were in pursuit, at a distance, but a distance that was definitely closing, and soon they were all beyond the reach of the house light. I stared into that darkness, my eyes examining every little eye floater as if it might manifest the movement of a body, or many bodies. I found none. I heard nothing. I returned here, to my seat. Before finding their place at the typewriter, my hands made work of the thread my aunt, in her chilling eagerness, had used to seal shut my shirt pocket. I am approaching.

When we left the home of the Philosopher's former student—she having told us to take the manuscript and leave, the Philosopher having then averted his eyes to the floor, remained silent, and shuffled out—I held the suitcase. I'd been the one to grab the last manuscript when we left, and the suitcase now held all three chapters. That I would then hand the full suitcase to the Driver was not so much a decision as an inevitability. Despite the either/ or of that depressive Dane, or the authentic/inauthentic binary of the man shuffling sadly before me down the hill, decisions of consequence never felt like the deliberation of one pregnant moment, time sharpened down like the tip of a pencil. Rather, the act of making a choice—in this case to hand the manuscripts to the Driver—seemed to happen in the body, not the conscious mind. It was an embodied act beyond thought, not unlike the swinging of a hammer. My choosing had already happened, it seemed, as I approached the waiting Driver at the automobile, in a process opaque to me. I realized, with mild horror, that I was not the active agent in my own thought process that I had imagined I was: Despite whatever language I could put to those processes, control still eluded me. I was a body carrying the manuscripts, a body whose mind had been, somewhere, made up. Even as my heartbeat increased its pace, I took great comfort in the sense not of deciding but of having already decided, and I now handed the suitcase to the Driver.

At the base of the hill, the Philosopher eyed the ground, reached directly for the door of the automobile. The security of his manuscripts was nowhere in his immediate concerns. As the Philosopher settled himself into a slump on the passenger seat, the Driver put the suitcase into the trunk. He closed the trunk and patted me on the back with surprising force. Seemingly confident that the Philosopher could not hear us, he said,

—My Compeer is housed just a few kilometers south of here. He will help us in what is to come.

I asked him what was to come, and he just said,

—We will see.

Then he told me that if, at any point in the drive to the Compeer's house, the Philosopher should attempt to wrest control of the steering wheel, it would be incumbent on me to wrest control of the Philosopher. This seemed to be a great advancement in commitment from my apparent decision to hand over the manuscripts, and yet it was not presented as a new decision to make because it was not a new decision to make. It was entirely enfolded into choices I had already made. If, as the Philosopher had written, the self was not a static entity but a continually unfolding process, then I seemed to be constantly running after the unfolding of my actual self, as if after a ball of yarn unrolling down a hill. In an attempt to get a few steps ahead, I was now imagining the scenario the Driver had laid out: In the event that the Philosopher, upon realizing that we would not be delivering him and his manuscripts back home, reached for the steering wheel, I would reach for him. Probably I would grab him first by the shoulders, shoulders that I now knew were not as full as they appeared in his suit jacket, but somewhat atrophic. I imagined the sensation of wool shoulder pads collapsing beneath my grasp, the sensation of wrapping my grip around clavicle and humerus, sinew and skin, as those arms tensed, muscles taut, in their attempt to grab the steering wheel from the Driver. Despite the Philosopher's unideal frame (his proportionality was less Vitruvian and more osteoporotic), I had seen at the Madam's house the surprising strength he possessed, and if I were unable to control his body, and the Driver had to fight for control of the steering wheel, there was a very real possibility that the struggle would send the automobile off the road, not into the forgiving, pillowing ditch of earlier but perhaps off a roadside cliff and into the billowing flames of our own immolation.

As we drove along, the space of my brain was ionized by thought but the air inside the automobile was untroubled by conversation. Not one of us seemed to regard or consider the others. We were three subjects, no objects. Three separate, non-intersecting subjectivities, then, approached a fork in the road. The fork was marked by a simple sign, legible in our headlamps, at the top of which two stubby arms directed us left to go south, right to go north. The pure potentiality of either/or. The Philosopher's gaze drifted to the road on the right. His body, too, drifted to the right, surely anticipating the imminent movement of the automobile. When, in a moment, the automobile would turn to the left, the panic and anger the Philosopher might feel—at his realization that he was, in effect, being abducted, at least for a time—would be my responsibility to contain. I readied myself. I positioned my body directly behind his. I placed my hands on the back of the passenger seat, ready to constrain him at his first outburst.

The Driver pulled the steering wheel to the left. The wheels turned south, and as we rumbled onto this new road, the Philosopher did not spasm with rage, did not shout profanity; he merely let his gaze linger on the sign as we drifted past. I saw his face in dark silhouette, behind him the trees illuminated by our headlamps, his mouth slack as if in an attempt to articulate what he no longer had the will to speak. He looked at the Driver and lowered his head like a scolded puppy. He then turned to look at me in the back seat. With the only light behind him, I could not see his face. But I saw enough to unclench my hands, unready my body for a struggle that would not occur. He slouched back into his seat. He said (I think),

—All right.

We drove until the trees became less dense. The fences of farmland reappeared, and we had to stop for a cow sitting on the road. The Driver cursed, got out, and seemed to plead with the cow to stand up and move. The Driver's body language was that of someone in intricate and tense negotiation; the cow's body language was that of a cow enjoying sitting in the road. The Philosopher and I watched this all. Neither of us moved to take control of the automobile and leave the Driver behind. It was simply not a possibility either of us seemed to entertain. Finally, the colloquy between the Driver and the cow ended, with the latter's intransigence proving the victor, and the Driver huffed back behind the wheel. He shifted back into gear and inched forward. The Driver propped himself up to peer over the hood as the bumper got closer to the cow. With the automobile moving at an aching creep, the bumper finally seemed to nudge the body of the cow. The Driver held his foot on the brake, still in the mode of negotiation; he'd made his move, and now it was time for the cow to make hers. I, unable to see much from the back seat, rolled down my window. Sticking my head out for a better view, I saw the cow look off into the night, not even bothering to grant us the acknowledgment of a glance. The Driver eased up on the brake just enough to let the engine idle us forward into another nudge in the rib of the cow. The response, while not a look of acknowledgment, much less a helpful retreat from the road, was still oddly satisfying: The cow flatulated. I pulled my head in and rolled my window back up.

—It occurs to me that after the herculean effort put into washing this automobile free of gore, it would be a shame to bloody it again.

That, to my surprise, was not me speaking, but the Philosopher. The Driver looked at our passenger with bemusement. The Driver sighed. Then he shifted into reverse. For a moment I thought this might be an opportunity for the

Philosopher to urge the Driver back to the north-heading road. Instead, the Philosopher pointed to the sloped grass on the side of the road and said,

—You can probably just go around.

And that's what the Driver did. As the automobile tilted along the grassy slope, we all tilted on our seats. With the cow behind us, I had nothing but our destination to consider. That brief standoff had been enough drama to distract me from the fact that we were on our way to the home of someone the Driver had referred to only as his Compeer, who presumably had plans for separating the Philosopher from his work. I placed my hand where the suitcase had been earlier, felt only itchy upholstery now. I could tell that a fume of the cow's gas had made its way into the automobile, was now lingering in invisible tendrils. I shooed it away with my hand. Soon, the Philosopher began shooing away the smell, too. And the Driver. We all, one by one, rolled down our windows. The night air was crisp, dry and crackly with pine. We all breathed it in, enjoyed the sound of road rolling beneath tires and forgot the circumstances of our silence. And then the Philosopher punctured that silence; it sounded like he'd suddenly sat on the entire horn section of an orchestra. The Philosopher said,

—Oh, dear God. I'm so terribly sorry.

He hunched down, seemed to examine the integrity of his trousers.

The Driver screamed,

—I thought that was the cow! But it was you the whole time?

With one hand on the steering wheel, he began waving frantically with the other. The Philosopher, his body crumpled in the corner of the passenger seat, said,

—It was the cow! At first.

The Driver barked, as if to both exhale the stench and express his disgust. He said,

—And then you thought you'd just, what, sneak your farts in too?

—I'm sorry.

The Philosopher hung his head into the open window, the gossamer of his hair resurrected in the wind. He eventually said,

—I suppose I thought my own contribution might mitigate that of the bovine.

This struck the Driver as funny, and a small chuckle soon avalanched into a hearty laugh, one that even compromised his ability to keep the front wheels true. The Philosopher seemed reassured by this response, and he added his own soft chuckles. Righting the automobile to the road, the Driver said,

—I'd say that's just about the best summation of your political philosophy. The Philosopher hesitated, then said he did not understand.

—As long as your shit don't stink as bad as the bigger ones, then you think no one should tell you to keep your asshole plugged.

Those were the last words for some time. Outside, the landscape, shallow, visible only in the light our automobile provided, did not seem to be something we moved through or into, but rather something that presented itself to us; details of nature appeared, approached, moved obligingly to the side, and disappeared.

The Compeer's farmhouse appeared to us as if on a conveyor belt, its high mansard roof festooned with little spires on either end like spikes on which to mount the heads of the vanquished. Of course, though, there were no heads. As we approached, up a long driveway, lights in the windows turned on. The driveway concluded in a roundabout just before the front porch. Mid-roundabout, the Driver came to a stop.

The front door of the house opened. I expected a large man to emerge. I wasn't sure why, but I was very certain that someone referred to as the Compeer should fill the space of that doorway with imposing authority. The body that emerged, though, was small, with a head much too large for the narrow shoulders beneath. The suit he wore struck me as odd at this time of night, unless its considerable wrinkles were proof that it was more bedwear than formalwear. As the Compeer approached, the Philosopher said,

—Could I telephone my wife?

And the Driver said,

—No.

A moment passed and he said,

—Wait here.

It was unclear if he was saying this to the Philosopher or to both of us. To be safe, I stayed in the automobile. The Driver got out to greet the hydrocephalic Compeer. The two embraced in a forceful hug. I averted my eyes from this intimacy, examined instead the patches of hair on the back of the Philosopher's neck. Two thick cords structured the skin of his nape, and I saw them stretch taut as he lowered his head again. I did not know at that point, though perhaps I should have guessed, that this would be the last time I would have a private audience with the Philosopher, and yet even if I had been aware of that, I doubt I would have done much about it. I searched the back of this man's head for evidence of the cathexis that had previously leashed me, but instead I just saw the back of a man's head: a liver-spotted scalp visible through sparse hair. The Philosopher's sigh had a slight tremor. He raised his head, but did not turn back to me, and he said,

—Your father was a farmer, you said?

I told him no, that my grandfather was. Outside, the Driver and the Compeer were engaged in a muted conversation that seemed to require mutual hunching.

—And his straw hat? You think his straw hat is the straw hat in *A Straw Hat*, yes?

—No, I said. I don't.

A cat crept along the crenellations of the mansard roof. The Philosopher said,

—But what if it is?

—It doesn't much matter.

That cat on the roof, in the light from the house, it looked familiar.

—You're a student, yes? Tell me, where do you study? I might know people there.

I pointed over his shoulder and asked him if he saw that cat, and if so if he thought that might be the Chemist's cat, the one that had come with us to the Madam's house, and, if so, how he thought it might have come here. The Philosopher said,

—Ah, all cats look the same. All cats are the same.

I sat for a moment with his sudden refutation of the entire body of thought that he had spent his career developing, and said,

—Huh.

He finally turned around in his seat to look at me, though his eyes were obscured in shadow when he said,

—Tell me where you study. I might know people there.

I wasn't sure why he was so insistent on this point. It seemed like such an odd way to try to impress me. I had already shown him how important his work had been to me; the fact that he knew people seemed incidental. But then, as the Compeer was approaching, the Philosopher looked back at him, then back to me and said,

—Tell them you know me.

Or he might have said,

—Tell them you knew me.

I don't know which. I think at the time, I heard *know*, but in the hours between then and now, I revisit it and hear *knew*. The more I think about it, the more certain I am that he said *knew*, not *know*, while conversely feeling like my every recall of that word moves me further from the actual utterance and toward something else, a facsimile that, no matter how much I hold it up to the light, is never the word itself.

Regardless, the Compeer knocked on the glass, leaned his face (mustache, underbite) up to the window, and said to the Philosopher,

—You will come with me now.

The Philosopher touched the door as if to get out, then stopped and turned back to me, and said,

—I have signed autographs, you know. People have asked for me to sign my books for them, and I have done it. Like a matinee idol. Would you like me to sign something for you? Do you have one of my books? I can sign it and you can show it to people.

I said no. I could no longer see the cat.

—Here, the Philosopher said. Give me a pen and I will give you an autograph for you to show people.

And he pulled at my shirt, attempting to reach into my sealed breast pocket. I jerked away from his grasping hands. I flailed at his flailing. I reached for the door and opened the door and pulled myself out and onto the ground and saw the feet of the Driver and heard his laughter too.

By the time the Driver was helping me get to my feet, the Compeer was helping or corralling the Philosopher out of the sedan. The Philosopher seemed unsteady on his feet. I, too, felt unsteady on my feet. Imagining how the Philosopher saw me, I had to imagine myself as the object of his subjectivity. I did not like that. Any part of it. I looked at the ground.

The Compeer began to lead the Philosopher away, down the walkway, around the house, to the detached garage. The Philosopher either seemed to have aged since I'd last seen him walk, or he was exaggerating the hitches in his gait for this new audience. I asked the Driver where the Compeer was taking him. The Driver said,

—He'll sleep out the night in that garage.

—And then you'll take him back home?

—It is uncertain. Ultimately, it's the manuscripts we want. We have a man in R—— who will know what to do with it all, all the papers.

—Will you destroy them?

—No. It's all evidence. It's all part of this. Part of how what happened happened. But our man in R—— will know what to do with the manuscripts.

—But why is that necessary? He's already Class Four. What about those trials? The classification system.

—It's all a farce. There's a thriving black market for papers confirming unaffiliated status. Those people then go work as they did before. In positions of influence. So when we see the fissures in the system, we fill them.

The Driver slapped me on the back.

—Would you like some tea?

The Compeer and the Philosopher were now out of sight. I said,

—Yes. Desperately.

The Driver let me into the Compeer's house. The central gathering area was filled like a furniture store with plush sittables. They were circled for conversation, surrounded by walls lined with bookshelves chaotically filled. The coffee tables were still covered in mugs dreggy with grounds, tumblers with a finger each of melted beige ice. I sat in a chair that was either generously proportioned or a loveseat. Either way, it made me feel blissfully small. The Driver asked again if I wanted a cup of tea. I don't know if I responded, but the Driver left through the swinging door. Between two bookshelves hung a framed sketch of a woman in three-quarters profile. Looking obliquely away from the gaze of the artist and of the beholder, she was shaded as if emerging from the paper itself.

I wondered: If the Driver and his Compeer were truly only interested in the manuscripts, and they now had them, why were we not all on our way to our various homes? And then, grateful that my backside was no longer being buzzily massaged by the grinding tension between tire and road, though even in the cushy, sedentary armchair my muscles retained a vibrating sense memory of that relentless movement, I wondered: Did I care? I had been promised a chance to rest, the Philosopher's captivity surely just a practical choice to avoid his interference with the plan for his manuscripts. So what did I care about at that moment? To not see another body gorily explode or chemically implode. I applied myself to the platter of biscuits, the tepid tea that had a metallic tang. At some point both had appeared on the table in front of me, and the Driver was now standing above me, telling me there was a cot in the attic where I could rest off the night.

The woman in the sketch wore a bonnet that was a mess of doodles, a shirtwaist that had the geometry of an ice cream cone, but between those two ridiculous garments, their lines suggesting the angry scribbles of a child first, the intended apparel only second, her face—shadowed eyes, slight overbite, well-defined philtrum groove—did not seem to be constructed of graphite at all. No lines were visible, only the fine texture of skin doing coy things with the light.

The Compeer opened the front door, but lingered on the porch while he scraped his shoes clean, then entered. He made an all-vowel sound that might have been one of exasperation or resignation or something else entirely, then, stepping into the clutter of chairs, he said to me,

—Having an interesting evening?

For some reason, it did not immediately register to me that he was referring to all the events that had brought me to this moment, so I just said I was noticing that portrait. He said,

—Ah.

I sipped my tea, and somehow that was the last sip; apparently I'd been in dire need of some, and I asked him who it was in the sketch. He said,

—No one. Just a picture.

And that struck me as horribly unfair. Looking at the woman who wasn't real, I knew I'd failed to complete the task my aunt had assigned me. I had not succeeded in making more of me. So it's just us, my aunt and me, until it isn't. I looked away from the portrait and fingered the material of my shirt's breast pocket, searching for the contours of its contents like a child investigating a wrapped present. Realizing how foolish I must have appeared, I pulled my hand away from my chest and laced my fingers around the empty cup in my hands. The Compeer said,

—Who gave you that tea?

I looked up, said,

—He did.

I pointed to the Driver, only to realize that he'd left the room. The Compeer said,

—That's the stuff they give the soldiers. Guess you won't be falling asleep anytime soon.

The sudden syncopation of my heart might have been a response to what he said or the tea taking effect; either way, I was sweating. I needed to think. The Philosopher had promised that preceding thought is Being, something essential not defined by thought. And yet a mind is not a mind in isolation but only when it has an object of thought: subject contingent upon object, object contingent upon subject. How could both be? The Philosopher had promised resolution to this problem, promised that one—I—could access this Being that precedes thought, that I could think my way there. If only I noticed the right things. If only I noticed the right way. I had to place one word after another, notice what I notice, notice what I do not notice. One word after another.

I asked the Compeer if he was quite sure that the woman in the portrait was not real, but by that point, I realized, I'd left the Compeer behind, as the Driver was escorting me up a narrow flight of stairs to the attic. Once there (which is: here), he turned on for me a gas lamp. I saw the cot, a table, this table, a chair, this chair, a typewriter, this typewriter, the moon outside the mansard window (now a milky memory). I was still holding the platter of biscuits. In the typewriter was a sheet of paper on which someone had typed, *To whom it may concern, if I should be expired upon your reading this, please know—*

But the sentence had not been finished.

I set my platter beside the typewriter and asked the Driver what that was. He waved at it dismissively, said,

—A paranoid habit of his.

Presumably he meant the Compeer.

—When he thinks he's going to be disappeared he tries laying down his final words—to be found by who, me maybe, even though I would already know that man's final thoughts. You know what it would be? In the moment death takes him, his final thought will be: garlic soup. It's all he eats. He must think about it all the time. It smells foul, and he practically sweats the stuff. Did you smell him? Can you imagine being that man's only friend for three decades, a man who sweats garlic soup? If he finished that note, that last will and testament or whatever, it would probably just be a recipe for garlic soup, the degenerate. I love him, but he's a culinary degenerate. Anyway.

The Driver shrugged. I sat down at the typewriter, looked at the Compeer's note to an unknown reader—surely his future self, as you are mine. (As I approach the *now*, I eagerly anticipate the disclosure of Being, in all its tidy resolution).

The Driver slapped my shoulder. Initially frightened, I soon realized this was intended as a gesture of affection. He said,

—You did a good job. Before I retire, can I get you anything? What do you want?

I asked him to tell me his real name. He said,

—No names.

I agreed, then I asked for a ream of paper.

—I am serious, though. No names.

I nodded.

The sun is coming up. I was beginning to think I'd lost it somewhere. But there it lazily goes. The sunrise is smudging the bottom of my window with oranges and purples. The colors look somehow delectable, the clouds edible. The landscape beneath those clouds appears plain, a dirt field stretching out from the house, patched with wild grasses that blend eventually into the woods. It is clear from this vista that we are not as isolated here as I thought. Peeking up over the trees: a steeple, bits of other buildings. Beyond that, where the woods surge into foothills, swaths of road cut through the trees. I hear, but don't yet see, the puttering of an engine, the elasticity of the sound suggesting it's moving away. I hear a rooster. Or maybe a man mimicking a rooster, the *cock-a-doodle-do* so pronounced it could not possibly be authentic. Then again, the racket of life has always sounded to me counterfeit. My hands hurt, my fingers clenched clawlike. It hurts more to unclench them than to type. My back is also turning my whole body clawlike.

In the silence between sentences, I listen for others in the house. I am convinced I am alone. Even if others are sleeping, I would hear the grind of snores. But my sense of being alone is not just about the absence of other human noise; there is a way in which bodies fill a space. It occurs to me that if I am alone in this house, I might like to have another look at that framed sketch downstairs, the woman in three-quarters profile. The Compeer said it wasn't of a real person, and I want a closer look at what that looks like.

I see no vehicles left outside—nothing to take me—where?—where I need to go. It will be a long walk, a long walk with no clear direction and possible explosions. I would like to think that I can walk that road, that I can arrive, somewhere, in one piece, in whatever my totality of self is, though I don't know what that would look like.

My nervous fingers have finally got the better of my shirt's breast pocket and I've torn my aunt's thread loose, unsealed my dead man's pocket. This has caught the eye of the cat, whom I still have not named. With the thread, I have attempted something of a lasso, but the cat, initially intrigued by my tricks, has turned away, drawn instead to the sunrise. Now at the window, he stares out at the emerging day, the garish swirl of the sky, the tumorous clouds. The cool crispness of the night is starting to dull at the edges, the breeze coming in no longer serrated. The cat's tail hangs back into the room and coyly flicks the air.

I could take the cat, and I could leave, if only to bring something with me. But—there's the contents of my pocket, too. I have to check, my earthly token.

I have now checked. The pocket is empty. There is nothing.

My aunt will be waking up soon. She has the hat, the actual one. And she will need breakfast. She will need my help. She will need me. There is still much to do.

The cat is now investigating something just outside the window, his paw reaching out onto the roof. I imagine the roof has a layer of frost, and that the cat might find padding across those slats tactilely satisfying. He turns back to me, looks, sees something.

ACKNOWLEDGMENTS

This novel began when I randomly picked a book off a shelf, *At the Existentialist Café* by Sarah Bakewell, and on page 180 read about a short, late-night road trip that seemed worth pursuing.

The unnamed student of the first epigraph was quoted in Karl Löwith's *My Life in Germany Before and After 1933: A Report*, translated by Elizabeth King. The second epigraph appears in the novel *The Robber* by Robert Walser, translated by Susan Bernofsky. The third epigraph is spoken by Groucho Marx in the film *Horse Feathers*, directed by Norman Z. McLeod and written by S.J. Perelman, Bert Kalmer, Harry Ruby, Will B. Johnstone, and Arthur Sheekman.

I'm grateful for Katharine Haake's editorial insights and for everyone at What Books Press. Thank you, as always, to Diana and August.

KEVIN ALLARDICE is the author of five previous novels. He earned an MFA from the University of Virginia and more recently received a Jack Hazard Fellowship from the New Literary Project. Originally from California, he now lives with his family in Iowa City, Iowa.

WHAT BOOKS PRESS

AN IMPRINT OF

THE GLASS TABLE

COLLECTIVE

LOS ANGELES

All WHAT BOOKS feature cover art by Los Angeles painter, printmaker, muralist, and theater and performance artist GRONK. A founding member of ASCO, Gronk collaborates with the LA and Santa Fe Operas and the Kronos Quartet. His work is found in the Corcoran, Smithsonian, LACMA, and Riverside Art Museum's Cheech Marin collection.

As a small, independent press, we urge our readers to support independent booksellers. This is easily done on our website by purchasing our books from Bookshop.org.

WHATBOOKSPRESS.COM

2024

The Manuscripts
KEVIN ALLARDICE
NOVEL

Father Elegies
STELLA HAYES
POEMS

Slow Return
PAUL LIEBER
POEMS

Dreamer Paradise
DAVID QUIROZ
POEMS

How to Capture Carbon
CAMERON WALKER
STORIES

2023

God in Her Ruffled Dress
LISA B (LISA BERNSTEIN)
POEMS

Figures of Wood
MARÍA PÉREZ-TALAVERA
TRANSLATED BY PAUL FILEV
NOVEL

A Plea for Secular Gods: Elegies
BRYAN D. PRICE
POEMS

Nightfall Marginalia
SARAH MACLAY
POEMS

Romance World
TAMAR PERLA CANTWELL
STORIES

2022

No One Dies in Palmyra Ohio
HENRY ELIZABETH CHRISTOPHER
NOVEL

Us Clumsy Gods
ASH GOOD
POEMS

Skeletal Lights From Afar
FORREST ROTH
FLASH FICTION/PROSE POEMS

That Blue Trickster Time
AMY UYEMATSU
POEMS

2021

Pyre
MAUREEN ALSOP
POEMS

What Falls Away Is Always
KATHARINE HAAKE &
GAIL WRONSKY, EDITORS
ESSAYS

*The Eight Mile
Suspended Carnival*
REBECCA KUDER
NOVEL

Game
M.L. WILLIAMS
POEMS

2020

No, Don't
ELENA KARINA BYRNE
POEMS

One Strange Country
STELLA HAYES
POEMS

*Remembering Dismembrance:
A Critical Compendium*
DANIEL TAKESHI KRAUSE
NOVEL

Keeping Tahoe Blue
ANDREW TONKAVICH
STORIES

WHAT
BOOKS
PRESS

LOS ANGELES

Milton Keynes UK
Ingram Content Group UK Ltd.
UKHW040311181024
449757UK00005B/484